Without ~~persuasion, they began dancing.~~ The music was slow, soaring with violins. The shadows elongated Daniel's dark features. He looked proud and mysterious.

In her white gauze and bright jewelry, Annabel glittered. Daniel touched her earrings and made them swing. They were tiny cats suspended in repeating circles of gold. He seemed mesmerized by the pendulum action.

Look at me, not my jewelry, Annabel willed him.

He looked at her.

She recognized him.

Her friend Emmie had been boasting about him for weeks.

He was Daniel Madison Ransom.

Other Scholastic books
you will enjoy:

The Party's Over
by Caroline B. Cooney

Saturday Night
by Caroline B. Cooney

Winter Dreams, Christmas Love
by Mary Francis Shura

The Last Great Summer
by Carol Stanley

FORBIDDEN

CAROLINE B. COONEY

SCHOLASTIC INC.
New York Toronto London Auckland Sydney

No part of this publication may be reproduced in whole or in part, or stored in a retrieval system, or transmitted in any form or by any means, electronic, mechanical, photocopying, recording, or otherwise, without written permisison of the publisher. For information regarding permission, write to Scholastic Inc., 730 Broadway, New York, NY 10003.

ISBN 0-590-46574-0

12 11 10 9 8 7 6 5 4 3 2 1   3 4 5 6 7 8/9

Printed in the U.S.A.   28

First Scholastic printing, August 1993

FORBIDDEN

ONE

It was the fourth week in June.

In Manhattan, the jet set gathered. Among the rich and famous, one eighteen-year-old girl was also truly beautiful. Annabel Jayquith was rarely alone and was accustomed to having every eye upon her.

In southern Ohio, another eighteen-year-old girl sat by herself in a dull and shabby row house in a dull and shabby town, watching television. Jade O'Keeffe was always alone, and nobody ever watched her.

Instead, she watched them.

Jade was looking at the *Late Night News*. She had recorded it, as she had been recording the news ever since she found the papers in the lockbox. She had tape after tape of evening news. This was one of her favorites.

"Hello, Theodora," said Jade.

The nation's best-known anchorwoman

smiled out of the television set. Theodora's smile was famous for its cruel edge. Theodora liked to pry the truth out of people who wanted to keep it hidden.

"This time," said Jade, taunting, "*I'm* the one with the smile, Theodora. And you're the one trying to hide the truth."

She practiced holding her head like Theodora. Then she worked on her laugh. Theodora Jayquith's laugh was often compared to gunfire. People said that being laughed at by Theodora Jayquith was like standing in front of a submachine gun: It was metallic and it hurt.

On television, Theodora interviewed Jade's favorite rock band. Jade owned six of their releases. She'd never even been able to afford a general seating ticket at one of their famous concerts. And there was Theodora Jayquith, calling the men by their first names. Touching the drummer's shoulder intimately. Theodora's famous laugh spilled over like a bronze waterfall.

The remote control shook in Jade's hand. *"I hate you, Theodora."*

At first, talking to the face in the television, Jade had whispered. One-way conversation seemed evil and twisted. She had not wanted to risk being overheard.

But there was no one to hear. Jade's parents were dead. Jade did not particularly miss them.

The suddenness of the car accident shook her, but tears never came, and grief never surfaced.

"Theodora! Look at me!" Jade knew the tape by memory and timed her demand, so the woman on the screen did look at her. "While you are wearing your designer gowns," said Jade, "do you know what I am wearing? Clothes from K Mart, Theodora. While you dine at famous restaurants with famous chefs, do you know what I eat? Kraft Macaroni & Cheese, Theodora. When you laugh with your fabulous stars, do you know who my friends are? High school dropouts. My so-called boyfriend works at a car wash." Jade's heavily lipsticked lips twitched.

Jade often reran Theodora's interview with the British prime minister. Jade cared nothing about politics. But in that interview, Theodora said easily, as if it were an everyday thing, "When Princess Diana and I were shopping in Switzerland . . ."

"I could have had that life!" cried Jade. "I could have visited castles in England and mansions in Beverly Hills with you! I could have known a princess and a rock band. You cheated me out of them."

The advertising break came on the tape. Jade examined her reflection in the hand mirror she kept by the VCR. Jade shared Theodora's body and bones, but not her face. She had the same thin straight hair, cut exactly the way Theodora did, a sleek cap frosted like champagne. Jade had colored contact lenses, too, and now her eyes were the same glittery green.

Theodora returned to the screen, uttering one of her viciously amusing remarks. Everybody in the newsroom threw back their heads and laughed.

"You discarded me as if I were a paper wrapper off fast-food you finished eating, Theodora," said Jade. "You were sixteen. A year younger than I am now. You decided I was nothing but a mistake. I was just an unfortunate turn of events. The best thing to do with me was forget about me. So you gave me away, Theodora Jayquith! And what is worse, you gave me away *to ordinary people*."

Jade was no longer able to sit. She was on her feet, looming above the television. She looked ready to stomp on it, or put her fist through it.

"Would you like to know how I grew up?" she shouted at the television. "I, your daughter? Your only child? The one you have *never mentioned* on television or anywhere else? In poverty, Theodora. In dull, dingy poverty."

"Good night," said Theodora to the world. She was perfectly centered in the television, her glittering hair a halo around her face. Her earrings were immense; she never wore the same pair twice; she was famous for her earrings. These looked like torn watercolor paper dusted with diamonds.

The camera panned over the broadcasting room. Theodora swiveled, addressing the sports announcer.

The sportscaster knows her, thought Jade. While I, her daughter, do not.

She punched the television off as if shoving an ice pick into its heart.

"You and I, Theodora, are about to meet." Jade's smile was a perfect replica of the famous Jayquith smile, full of the relentless cruelty that uncovers lies. "You're going to pay, Theodora," she whispered, shivering with desire. "Everything you have will be mine!"

TWO

People "collected" Annabel Jayquith. Strangers clipped stories about her out of celebrity magazines, keeping scrapbooks and chatting about her as if they were old friends. Annabel didn't mind the photographs. It was the print that made her queasy. Since Annabel's father did not permit her to talk with reporters, the papers had to make things up. Nothing was too ridiculous or exaggerated for the tabloids. They would write anything to sell copies.

A billionaire's daughter is always at risk. It was not unknown for Hollings Jayquith to hire guards for Annabel, who would watch for the gate crashers, the crazies, or the homicidal.

Her eighteenth birthday party had taken place in the Mirror Hall of a French palace. Guests were flown in from around the world, every one in royal French court costume. The men and boys were as glorious in their peacock satins as the women. In this gathering of "the beautiful people," most were rich or famous or both. But Annabel *really* was beautiful. In her iridescent dress with its frosting of flowers, she was as haunting as an unobtainable jewel. Her skin was alabaster white, her hair an avalanche of pure black. To the public fascinated by her, Annabel equalled romance.

Her birthday portrait, in which a hundred lovely Annabels seemed to dance within the mirrors, ended up on the cover of *Famous*, and from that issue, she *became* famous. Overnight there was an Annabel look in fashion, Annabel hairstyles, even Annabel figures. She expected to be famous like an Olympic skater or gymnast, her star eclipsed in a few years. But her friends pointed out that while athletes slipped from first place, Jayquiths would always be rich.

At that night's charity ball, she did not remotely resemble the *Famous* photograph. The fund-raising dance was held in the Egyptian Wing of the Metropolitan Museum of Art in New York. Annabel could not resist the chance to be an Egyptian princess. She and her hairstylists spent a wonderful afternoon sorting through color photographs of Nefertiti and Ankhesnamun, deciding how to braid Annabel's black cloud of hair. Somebody had been sent out to get gold cords and bright stones to weave like

a bejeweled harness into a hundred thin braids.
Annabel arrived at the ball dressed like Pharoah's
daughter in pleated white linen. Her jewelry
shone with beaten gold, brilliant blue lapis lazuli,
and deep red rubies. Her eyelids were painted
like Cleopatra's. She looked stunning, but she
did not look like Annabel Jayquith.

Usually Annabel would be with her father at
such an event, but he was in Japan on business, and instead she was with the Bruce-
Newcombes, whom she barely knew and did
not want to know better. Mrs. Bruce-Newcombe wore black, the color in which New
Yorkers specialized. She was adorned with a famous necklace, whose history she told Annabel
twice.

Annabel disappeared into the shadows before
she had to dance with Mr. Bruce-Newcombe.
Luckily, since the Temple of Dendur was lit by
torchlight for the occasion, there were plenty of
shadows. She had no guards. She was, after all,
with the Bruce-Newcombes.

The vast room in which the ancient Temple
of Dendur had been rebuilt echoed with the clat-
ter of twentieth-century shoes on stone. Annabel
held herself tall and regal, and sometimes even
sideways. Walk like an Egyptian, she sang to
herself, pretending to be Queen Nefertiti painted
on a pyramid wall. But Nefertiti had had her

king. Annabel had only strangers to dance with. Don't think about it, Annabel told herself. Princesses are not lonely.

She danced for an hour. Annabel never tired of dancing but she certainly tired of partners her father's age. Time to retreat.

She slid into the darkness, easing down behind a floor vase large enough to hold a mummy. A stone ledge let her sit with her knees drawn up, her gold sandals half-tucked under the sharp creases of her gown.

Before her was the reflecting pool, black and ghostly in the torchlight, decorated with papyrus as if it were the Nile. Guests who possessed millions of dollars — guests who had given twenty-five thousand of them to come here tonight — threw pennies into the pool, making wishes.

There is nothing, thought Annabel, that they cannot buy. Nothing they don't already own. And look at them! Finding a penny, holding it tight, making a wish, watching it sink.

I know what they wish for . . . what I wish for . . . what we all wish for . . . to love and to be loved.

Every one of us here is hoping that tonight will be the night.

Loneliness hit Annabel like a smart bomb. No! No! She actually held up a hand against it. I don't want to feel lonely tonight.

But loneliness, which has a mind of its own, came anyway, programmed to attack the vulnerable corners of her heart.

She had been lonely at Wythefield Academy, which never seemed possible even when it was happening. There would be her roommate Emmie Pearse giggling in the next bed, reading aloud from celebrity magazines. (Emmie adored Annabel's fame. Emmie subscribed to the magazines the Jayquiths hated, like *People* and *Us* and *Famous* and *Personality*. Then she liked to visit Annabel in New York and listen to Annabel's Aunt Theodora tell what the celebrities were really like.) There would be Annabel, cross-legged on the floor, studying Milton or physics, two subjects that very nearly ruined her senior year.

And there would be loneliness, joining them like a third roommate. Of all the subjects they discussed in their four years as roomies, they never once talked about loneliness. How could you sit with your closest friend, and admit that in spite of her friendship, you were lonely?

Besides, the Wythefield girls had voted Annabel's father Most Attentive, Most Willing to Have the Entire Class Visit. How could you claim loneliness with a father who showered you with phone calls, faxes, and jewelry? She was in school with girls who, after ugly divorces, hadn't heard from their fathers in years. With girls whose fathers hardly remembered their names.

Hollings Jayquith was ferocious, and a little frightening, and the most interesting man on earth. People could say what they wanted about Hollings — and they did; his reputation was not angelic — but not one of the four hundred girls at Wythefield had a father as wonderful as Annabel's, though he was rarely home. His business covered the globe, and he liked to materialize at every office, every factory, and every mine. He had great energy, and found it unbearable to sit around doing nothing. Or even sit around doing something. His private jet had Nautilus equipment so he could work out during long flights. He was always on the telephone to Annabel, or sending her presents, or expressing a piece of jewelry he had spotted in a shop window in Switzerland or Singapore.

As for Aunt Theodora, her home was the television studio. She loved dealing with the eternally famous, or the temporarily famous. She loved knowing that one of the definitions of fame was whether or not you had been on Theodora Jayquith's show. Theodora passed through Annabel's world tossing glamor like confetti.

Hollings and Theodora loved Annabel. They told her constantly that she was the center of their lives.

But Annabel knew their work was.

If Mama had lived, Annabel liked to tell herself, I would have been at the center of *her* life.

Of course she couldn't prove that. Her mother had painted and collected paintings. Maybe as the years went by, the center of Mama's universe would have been art, and not Annabel. Maybe Annabel was lucky Mama had died young, because she never had to face the truth that she could be second even for her mother.

It was Annabel's dream to be the center of somebody else's life. She did not tell that to Aunt Theodora, who believed that your inner core of strength should be enough. You should enjoy other people, but enjoy yourself most.

Even though Jayquith women had gone to Wythefield for four generations, every now and then loneliness undercut Annabel's faith in Hollings and Theodora. Had they sent her to Wythefield so she would be somebody else's responsibility? So they could schedule the motherless child for vacations only?

Annabel wanted to spend her life with one man who would think his entire existence was a vacation because he was with her.

Dim and insubstantial in the flickering light,

a once famous actress and her elderly husband
dropped pennies into the pool. They had been
married for four decades. How lucky, thought
Annabel, to grow old together.

Annabel was a closet grave-visitor. When she
turned sixteen and was given her own cars, the
first journey she took by herself was to the cemetery where her mother had been laid to rest
when Annabel was nine. She had had great ex-
pectations. Here, by the quiet stone, with three
words and two dates, she hoped to hear her
mother speak. But Eleanor Taft Jayquith remained silent. The answers Annabel wanted, she
had to compose herself.

And yet it was extraordinarily peaceful to visit
her mother's grave. If Annabel went weeping,
she left serene. If she went happy, she left joyful.

She had not been there in weeks. Too busy.
Final exams, graduation from Wythefield, shopping for the perfect dress for each summer event,
bridal showers for her roommate Emmie's older
sister Venice. Emmie would be maid of honor
and Annabel was one of the ten bridesmaids. By
far the nicest thing about Venice's wedding was
that Venice's mother was enjoying it so much.
Annabel loved seeing Mrs. Pearse, because Mrs.
Pearse was seeing only love.

True love, thought Annabel. I'd like to know
where mine is and what's taking so long. If I

had a mother, we'd talk about love. We lost it all, Mama and I. No hugs, no good-night kisses. We shared no pain, told no stories. She won't help plan my wedding and she won't weep when I come down the aisle.

Sometimes when Annabel went to her mother's grave, she wondered if her mother had had enough love. With Daddy so frequently away, so deeply involved in the financial empire he had built, had Mama been loved enough?

Would Venice and Michael, getting married next Saturday, have enough love to go around?

Venice had actually wanted one of those athletic weddings where the bride and groom compete first in the New York Marathon, with a priest waiting at the finish line, and then celebrate by bungee jumping off the Brooklyn Bridge. Michael said his wedding would be in a church on a village green, with the usual flowers, long gowns, and champagne. Venice gave in. If that wasn't true love, Annabel didn't know what was.

I could be like Aunt Theodora, thought Annabel. She never married. Domestic life bores her. She likes conversation, fashion, jewels, and jets. The men in her life aren't even handsome or tall. They're powerful. Like Daddy.

Annabel's father-adoration worried Aunt Theodora. "What man will measure up to Hollings?" she would say. "Who will we ever find for you?"

If Aunt Theodora — to whom prime ministers and presidents, rock stars and movie moguls, trendsetters and late night comics came begging for screen time — couldn't find the right man for Annabel, then who could?

Suddenly it was imperative to make a wish in this pool, this Nile, this night. Her tiny evening bag, hanging almost invisibly from a single gold string, contained only tissues and lipstick. Annabel stood up. The gauzy princess gown was tied high above her waist with a thick gold cord, and then fell in scores of sharp pleats to her ankles. Wearing it was remarkably different from wearing jeans. She felt — and was — half-exposed.

Next to her, shadowed by the alabaster vase, stood another guest. He was nothing to Annabel but striped trousers and gleaming shoes. "Excuse me," said Annabel. The forgotten braids swung heavily around her chin. It was so strange to have weighted hair. "Would you lend me a penny, please?"

"Lend?" he repeated. His laugh was young. One chuckle and she wanted to see his face. What features went with a great laugh like that?

"So, we'll meet again, you and I?" he teased. "And you'll return my penny?"

"Absolutely. I don't want you in financial difficulties." She circled so that the flickering torch-light would illuminate his face. He was in his twenties. He had thin satiny hair, fierce eyes, and big hands. He was not all of a piece, like some men; he was no magazine model. He was more. He was the kind of man to whom Aunt Theodora was drawn. How young he was, to give off an aura of power.

She knew him from somewhere, which was no surprise, because she knew all these people from somewhere. It was always the same people who had money to give: These were the ones who donated their art collections or their estates, who wrote the huge checks. She had met these people last month at an AIDS fund-raiser and would run into them again when they did International Relief. But she could not immediately put a name to this man's face.

She did not tell him her name, either. The braids and the Cleopatra eye shadow would not give a clue to the romantic French princess she had been on the cover of *Famous*.

There was a certain thrill in using her famous last name. Sometimes she loved to watch a person's face as connections were made. *Jayquith?* the eyebrows would say. *Hollings* Jayquith? the lips would move. *His* daughter? *Theodora* Jay-quith? *Her* niece?

It could be fun.

But nobody knew better than Annabel the price you could pay for a last name. Taught the hard way by school events, tennis club matches, and hunt club weekends, she knew that once the two syllables of her last name were uttered, everything was irrevocably changed. Nothing could be ordinary. Nothing could be casual. People wanted to know what it was like to be so wealthy. They wanted to know about Aunt Theodora, what was she really like, whether Annabel, too, had met the incredible array of celebrities who paraded in and out of Theodora's life every day. People wanted invitations. They wanted to stand uncomfortably close, as if fame and wealth really did rub off. They wanted to touch her, as if they planned to take some of her for a souvenir.

Annabel wanted this man to think only of her. So when he said "I'm Daniel," she said, "I'm Annabel." She held her breath. A woman would have known there was only one Annabel. But she was safe. To him, it was only a name.

Daniel fished in his pockets. Annabel loved how men filled their pockets. She loved his hand, too big for the pocket. She loved his smooth cool palm, full of pennies waiting for her to choose.

She took the oldest penny, the one that looked

as if it had experience, and had been around the
world. She didn't want any shiny new amateur
penny. She wanted one to make the wish come
true.

> Wish I may, wish I might
> Have the wish I wish tonight . . .
> *True love.*

She wanted to whisper out loud, leaning into
the *sh* and the *t* — an incantation. As if, like
Pharaoh's daughter, she was surrounded by
priestesses who could turn alligators into gods.
But she didn't want the young man to laugh at
her.

It turned out that one wish was not enough.
She took a second penny, and then a third. Each
penny she gripped with such intensity she could
hardly bear to let go. They fell slowly through
the water, and then lay on top of the others,
indistinguishable. Get to work, Annabel told the
pennies.

Daniel handed over pennies until he had none
left. "What's your wish?" he asked finally.
"Must be important." His hand, now empty of
change, rested comfortably on her waist, as if it
had always been there and always would be.

His voice was melodious. Made for duets,
thought Annabel, and blushed in the dark. If she

told this poor guy she was already planning duets, he'd be out of the Egyptian Room faster than King Tut on a chariot. "That would be telling," said Annabel. "The wish might not come true."

He grinned. At first she had not thought he was handsome, but now she changed her mind. People said you could look into a soul through the eyes, but Annabel disagreed. You looked in through the smile.

"Let's dance," said Daniel. "I love dancing, don't you?"

The drama of the dark and the intensity of the wishes evaporated. She was just a pretty girl with an adorable boy who'd asked her to dance.

"Alternatively," said Daniel, sounding younger and younger, "we could eat. I like eating more than anything. You're not on a diet, are you? I hate girls on diets. One quick shove into the Nile for you if you're on a diet."

Annabel promised that she was not now, never had been, and never intended to be on a diet. They walked through the papyrus to find the buffet. "We name our cats after rivers," he told her. "We actually have a cat named Nile. We used to have Amazon and Mississippi, too, but they had a bad habit of sleeping in the road."

"Oh, no!" said Annabel. "I love cats. You should have kept them indoors."

"Do Amazon and Mississippi sound like indoor cats to you?"

"Good point."

The light was better around the food tables. Annabel feasted her eyes on Daniel while he loaded her plate with cakes and pastries.

"Are you supposed to look like Pharaoh's daughter?" said Daniel. "If so, you win."

"You, however, are not wearing a loincloth."

"Sure I am. Hidden under the cummerbund." He added a honeycake to her plate. Annabel suppressed a desire to lick the honey off his sticky fingers. Get a grip, she told herself, but of course she didn't, and instead began gathering clues from Daniel. "Are you in college?" she asked. Annabel could hardly wait to go to college herself. She was crossing the continent. It felt as if she were crossing some great divide in her life as well. Sometimes she was out of breath just thinking of the leap it would involve.

"Just graduated." He dismissed the four years without names or description. "How about you?"

She smiled. "Just graduated. But from Wythefield." So they were four years apart. That was good. Annabel found boys her age annoying. They could only talk about cars, stereo systems, or sports. Annabel had a limited interest in all three.

Annabel felt the eyes of the gathering upon them. She was used to it, and knew how to maintain a private conversation in the midst of a crowd, but with Daniel, she did not want a crowd. She wanted true privacy. "You need to make a wish, too, Daniel."

Daniel nodded, accepting her suggestion. Pennies gone, he used a quarter. "That means my wish is worth twenty-five of yours," he told her. Then he surprised her. Staring at the silver coin as if it held some five-thousand-year-old truth from the real Temple of Dendur, he threw his quarter with unexpected violence. It splashed down far away. He, too, watched it sink, and the muscles in his jaw, the tendons in his throat, tightened.

Annabel approved. Hollings Jayquith had that fierce approach. You would never find her father absently dropping a penny in the water. He hurled himself into life. He never let things fall where they might. "What's your wish?" she said.

"I have a mission."

Bad word. Was he too religious? An environmental fanatic? A political freak? Now that she thought about it, this particular fund-raiser might draw the fanatics of the world. "A mission?" she repeated dubiously. She wanted Daniel to be flawless.

But Daniel did not discuss his mission. He changed the subject. "What are you doing this summer?" he asked her.

Dreaming of college, actually. Sometimes when she thought about the courses she would take, the friends she would have, and the freedom she would exercise, Annabel had to break into dancing and clapping. Love her father and aunt though she did, she was headed for the opposite coast. At college she would be a woman, not a girl; an adult, not an obedient boarding school child; studying for a career, not grades. And in August she would work at Aunt Theodora's network, a summer intern supposedly treated like any other summer intern. "Nothing special," she said, although she expected every day of summer to be special. "A little travel. Some tennis." She didn't want to talk about anything serious now. "How about you?"

"Just hanging around, resting up for law school." He was smiling again. He must be looking forward to law school.

Everybody at this kind of party spent the evening smiling, but their smiles meant nothing. Whether or not you were having fun, the rules said you must smile widely and continually. Daniel's smile was real. She had the odd sensation of wanting to possess his smile, the way she possessed yachts and town houses. She had to look away, lest he read her thoughts. "Let's do something tonight," she said, falling into his smile.

"Most people," Daniel told her, "would call a charity ball at the Egyptian Room doing something."

"Boring charity, though."

"Difficult to get interested in Mr. Thiell's hobby," agreed Daniel, laughing. "Have you ever visited one of his wildlife preserves?"

"I thought they were wrapped up with flesh-slicing wire to keep visiting human beings out." Her Aunt Theodora's long-time escort, J Thiell, owned gambling casinos from Nevada and the Dakotas to New Jersey and the West Indies. In an attempt to polish his image, Mr. Thiell had taken up a fashionable cause. The environment. Trees. Green space. He would buy big old abandoned factories and whatever acreage went with them. Then he'd demolish the buildings and turn the grounds into one of his Wildlife Preserves.

"The Preserves are so small," said Daniel, "that I always wonder just what wildlife he's preserving."

"Chipmunks."

Daniel laughed. "Grasshoppers."

Without discussion, they began dancing. The music was slow, soaring with violins. The shadows elongated Daniel's dark features. He, too, looked like an Egyptian painted on a wall, proud and mysterious.

In her white gauze and bright jewelry, she glittered every time she passed under a torch. Daniel touched her earrings and made them swing. They were tiny cats suspended in repeating circles of gold. He seemed mesmerized by the pendulum action.

Look at me, not my jewelry, Annabel willed him.

He looked at her.

She recognized him.

Emmie had been boasting about him for weeks.

He was Daniel Madison Ransom.

THREE

Even Annabel Jayquith was thrilled.

Who in America had not followed the life of Daniel Madison Ransom? Emmie had been wildly excited when the Pearses found out that Daniel Madison Ransom would be an usher at Venice's wedding. When Emmie found an article about Daniel in one of her celeb magazines, even Annabel read it twice.

A boy made famous by one fact: His father had been murdered.

Senator Madison Ransom and his wife, Catherine, had truly been among the beautiful people. She was honey-blonde and he was mahogany-dark. Lithe and athletic, they dressed in the casual way of people who came into the world perfect, and to whom the world was perfect in return. Every talk show wanted the Ransoms. Theodora must have interviewed them together or separately a dozen times. The senator and his

wife were articulate, idealistic, and decent. It was
the decency that drew America to them. There
had been much talk about Senator Ransom becoming President of the United States when he
was older and more seasoned.

It was Catherine who made The Camp famous. Catherine Ransom engineered the architecture to evoke Abe Lincoln. Even though The
Camp was twenty sophisticated rooms of lake-
front, you would have thought the Ransoms and
their sweet little boy Daniel were actually pi-
oneers in a one-room log cabin. Plenty of people
called their summer homes "camps," but only
Catherine got away with it.

When the senator hosted a meeting between
the Russian premier and the British prime minister, America went crazy. If owning a house
made of logs turned you into a president, Senator
Ransom would have been elected that afternoon.

Instead he was murdered.

A few months after the historic Camp Con-
ference, when America hung on every word he
uttered, Senator Madison Ransom took the floor
of the Senate. He had previously announced —
through Theodora Jayquith — that he was
going to expose an entire, unnamed industry.
He would prove he was presidential material.

Senator Ransom wrote his own speeches, used
no notes, and had no text. At last — a politician

without a squadron of speech writers. Madison Ransom stood before the Senate, his wife and son proudly in the gallery. His future, and theirs, seemed assured.

When the shots rang out, the chaos was incredible. Senators dived for safety. Security sprang into position. Screams ricocheted as loudly as bullets. Twelve-year-old Daniel Ransom watched his father die.

Only moments later, the killer was also killed, shot by the police as he fled the building. His body was never identified; his fingerprints were unknown. And most of all, his motive was unknown. Had he had a grudge? Was he crazy? Had he been hired?

No one knew.

Nor did anyone know the content of the speech that Senator Ransom never made. He had wanted complete surprise. No leaks. No escape route for the people he was about to slug.

The funeral was as impressive as if Madison Ransom really had been president. Dignitaries from around the world and the nation came to walk behind the casket. Daniel, tears running down his cheeks, was filmed every step of the way. He was a small twelve-year-old, frail and appealing. Every woman in America wanted to comfort this sad little boy.

It was the kind of death that attracted everybody: a romantic murder. Reporters never tired of writing shallow articles about the assassination and producers were always glad to make yet another TV special.

America's television and magazines followed the child with greedy fascination. Daniel Ransom was lucky; he did well in life. The coverage would have been a nightmare if he had failed. He grew bigger, for which he was grateful. He ceased to be pretty and he photographed poorly. This did not in any way stop the photographers from following him everywhere.

The world saw young Ransom crewing in an America's Cup race at sixteen; attending Wimbledon tennis championships; partying with movie stars, and eating at the latest trendy restaurants with Broadway playwrights. Daniel did not look at the photographers who chased him, nor would he answer the reporters' questions.

Not one interview did the widow or the son ever give — not even to Theodora Jayquith, who had practically sponsored the senator's fame.

Daniel Madison Ransom! Those, thought Annabel Jayquith, were powerful pennies. The one other person my age who would understand the liability of a famous last name. The one other person who dreads introducing himself. In Daniel's case, no doubt, people would insist on tell-

ing him where they had been and what they had
been doing at the moment his father was killed.
A person would tire of that.

They slipped behind the great stones, through
the dark and echoing chambers, and found their
way out of the museum and onto the street. She
wondered what her father would do to her when
the Bruce-Newcombes told him that she'd left.

She shivered and Daniel slipped his jacket off
his shoulders and onto hers. Its lining, rich with
his scent and his shape, caressed her bare arms.

Last year, *New York* magazine had listed Daniel Madison Ransom among its sexiest bachelors.
Annabel would vote for that. In fact, she *had*
voted for that — the senior Wythefield dorm ran
its own annual Sexiest Bachelor poll. She'd
voted for Daniel last January, wondering
vaguely why their paths had never crossed.

Now their paths had crossed.

The world of the fabulously wealthy was very
enclosed. Even so, it was an astonishing coinci-
dence.

You don't even know who I am, Daniel, Annabel said to him silently, but you're scheduled
to walk down the aisle with me next Saturday.
You are a friend of the groom and I am a friend
of the bride.

The sidewalk had been hosed down. It
gleamed wetly in the dark. The immense mu-

seum rose up behind them like a palace in France. Daniel signaled a taxi. The driver grinned from ear to ear when he saw Annabel. "Like your dress. Where you going in that dress?"

She'd forgotten how exotic she looked. Where was she going? She would certainly stand out.

"I know a place," said Daniel, helping her into the taxi.

They held hands. She could feel his fingerprints. She read his whorls and curls as if she were the FBI.

We'll be connected forever, Annabel told herself. Our fingerprints will grace the same glass and our hands will sign with the same pen.

There had been enough insurance money to bury her parents, pay off their silly credit card charges, buy herself the expensive colored contacts and the wardrobe she desperately hoped was correct, and a one-way plane ticket. Jade hated Theodora for giving her away to such feckless people. They didn't even have decent life insurance. Ten thousand dollars. What was that supposed to do?

Jade had little left. Either she pulled this off quickly or . . .

Well, she was Jade. She would pull it off quickly. Period.

She had not locked the door behind her when

she left Ohio, since there was nothing in the house Jade now cared about or ever had. A taxi took her to the airport limousine service where she was deeply disappointed to find that the "limousine" was just a bus. She had expected to sit in the back, behind a chauffeur, on deep soft leather seats, with a tiny TV, a telephone, and a real bar. A particularly ordinary person took the seat next to her, in spite of the fact that Jade had carefully covered the seat with her purse and magazine.

Ordinary people follow me everywhere. I cannot get rid of them. Theodora doesn't put up with this. Her limousine is a limousine. And she is literally jet set. Has her own plane. Flies everywhere.

Even the plane was not the stuff of which dreams were made. Passengers were seated three abreast, and the people on either side of her were fidgety and talkative and the man smelled of cigarettes and the woman of cheap perfume.

Jade did not spend the first flight of her life wondering what it would be like to be a pilot or a hostess. She did not look out the window to watch America passing beneath her. She thought only of landing.

New York. Where it would all begin.

New York did not let her down. From the horse carriages gathered near the Jayquith Hotel at Central Park to the white and gray and black stretch limousines that drifted past the uniformed doormen, from the windows at Tiffany's to the gowns at Bergdorf Goodman, New York was as awesome and splendid as she had known it would be.

The lobby of the hotel alone was worth the trip. Its ceiling was as far away as the spire of a church. It rippled and sparkled with as much gold as palaces. The people who worked there wore uniforms like the Queen's Guard and the flower arrangements spread as wide and as dramatic as Cinderella's gown. People spoke in soft voices — not library voices; not fear of being heard — but with the assurance that they did not need to raise the volume in order to be obeyed.

Jade could not, however, afford the Jayquith Hotel or anything like it. She ended up in an ugly place with utilitarian bedspreads and a television bolted to the wall. It was full of other people who couldn't pay for a nice place, either. She hated all their jabbering excitement at seeing New York.

I won't have to put up with this for long, she told herself. I will live in my own suite at the Jayquith, just like Theodora.

Twenty-four hours later, she knew better.

First she tried to get to the twelfth floor of Jayquith Corporate Headquarters, which con-

tained the television studios. The guards lounging in the lobby rested their palms on the guns
they carried on their hips. She explained that she
was Theodora Jayquith's daughter. "Please give
Miss Jayquith this message," said Jade. "I have
come."

The guards did not even laugh at her. "Get
out, kid."

"I really am! You have to let her know I'm
here!"

"Our job is to keep the nutcases away, not
make introductions."

"Listen to me!" cried Jade. "I have proof. I
can — "

"Don't make us get rough, kid. Buzz off."

Failing at the studio, she tried the Jayquith
Hotel. Jade was escorted out of the building the
moment she asked to see Miss Jayquith. She circled the block and came in another entrance, only
to be met by the same uniforms who had removed her a minute before.

"Please," she said, "I have to see Miss Jayquith. It's very important."

"Right," said the uniforms sarcastically, and
led her back to the sidewalk.

Next Jade telephoned.

A voice said, "Jayquith Hotel, how may I help
you?"

The moment she told them how they could

help her, they disconnected. They had no intention of helping her. The world was full of sickos who used any excuse in the world to get near a star, and Jade's story of being Theodora's daughter was instantly dismissed. But I have proof! thought Jade.

It had not occurred to her that nobody would even bother to look at her proof.

In despair and rage she went to the only place that seemed safe enough to sit down in — the New York Public Library.

The reference librarian whipped out a volume called *How to Find the Rich and Famous*. Alphabetical order — hundreds of show business people, their street and business addresses, their summer house and ski chalet addresses.

Theodora had four listings:

Jayquith Building — phone number of the main switchboard that had already refused to speak with Jade.

Jayquith Hotel — phone number of the front desk that wouldn't give her the time of day.

Eleven Levels Road, Litchfield, Connecticut. No phone number.

Pink Roof House, Bermuda. No phone number.

Much as Jade would like to visit Bermuda, that would have to wait until Theodora took her. But Eleven Levels Road, Litchfield, Connecticut, sounded possible. The phone number, of course, was unlisted. Fine. She'd just drive there.

She bought a map, located Litchfield and went to rent a car. "Under twenty-one?" said the rental people. "Nope. Gotta be twenty-one."

She called the train station. No train went remotely near Litchfield. Called the bus station. No buses, either. But the man said, "It's a resort, isn't it? See if a tourist agency runs a day trip."

The answer was at her own ugly hotel. The desk fixed her up with a tour. She would be forced to visit a Flower Farm, whatever that was, have lunch at some country inn, and finally arrive in Litchfield for two hours of "walking on the green," whatever that was, too.

If they won't let me in the front, I'll come in the back, thought Jade.

And what if she didn't? What if, after all, there was no entrance to Theodora's world?

Her hatred hardened like a diamond that could cut through glass.

Daniel Madison Ransom and Michael Thiell had become friends in the way of college boys who are not talkers. They did things together. They skied, played squash and tennis, went sailing, were partners in car rallies, traveled in California and Europe. The only thing they had never done together was study, because Michael had not the slightest interest in school.

"You have to study," he told Daniel, "because you'll grow up to take your father's old Senate seat. I can skip all that."

Michael skipped everything he could. It was his way of rebelling against his own famous father, J Thiell, whom he avoided whenever possible. Not that avoidance was necessary. He rarely even knew where his parents were living. Every year or so, each of his parents liked to acquire a new spouse and a few new residences. They might winter in Italy or summer in Norway, spend Christmas in Mexico or Thanksgiving in Hawaii. Michael was not usually invited along. Michael had spent many holidays with Daniel, but Daniel had never visited Michael.

The only constant in J Thiell's life was Theodora Jayquith, who fascinated him. Between wives — or even during wives — J Thiell liked to be seen with a Jayquith.

Yet Michael loved the idea of marriage. He wanted a traditional stable, solid marriage. He yearned to start his own family. He all but took notes when he visited other people's families, so he could see how it was done.

Daniel understood that. He wanted Michael to have it, and wanted to be in the wedding party. Nevertheless, Michael's choice was mys-

tifying. Venice Pearse was one unfeeling
woman. Difficult to imagine wanting to be
around her full-time.

But then, Daniel had an unfeeling woman of
his own to contend with. His mother. Catherine
Ransom appointed Daniel to take his father's
place when he was only twelve. Her demands
never ended. Her interest in his life was so intense that sometimes Daniel could hardly bear
to answer the phone, let alone go home for a
weekend.

Daniel's mother had never remarried. Instead
she made a career of being Senator Ransom's
widow. Daniel felt she enjoyed being the widow
as much as she had enjoyed being the wife. And
the next career with which she dealt was Daniel's: He was to follow in his father's path.

Like child stars in television, he had been a
child star at political events. Daniel wanted medical school. He loved babies and small children,
and hoped to be a pediatrician. It sounded like
a wonderful life, as close to normal as he would
get. His mother insisted on law, which would
lead to politics, which would put a Ransom back
in the Senate.

Daniel had read biographies of famous mili-
tary men, and discovered that great generals like
MacArthur had mothers who actually moved to

West Point to monitor their sons. He sympa-
thized. His mother's main home was in Man-
hattan, and she also kept a winter house in Boca
Raton, The Camp in Massachusetts, and when
Daniel went to Harvard, she bought a place in
Cambridge.

Nearly ten years had passed since his father's
murder. Catherine Ransom, whose self-imposed
loneliness had lasted so long, wanted to celebrate
the murder anniversary the way a normal
woman would celebrate her wedding anniversary. Catherine Ransom wanted a party . . . at
which she would expose the murderer.

Two Senate committees had failed to uncover
anything. But Catherine went to work, after all
that time, and found a single fact. Working from
that, she uncovered two more. Three little pieces
of knowledge, but Catherine — and now Daniel, too — knew who had ordered the killing of
Senator Ransom.

Proving it to the world, let alone judge and
jury, would be harder.

Catherine swung from one terrible mood to
a worse one, obsessed even more by the anniversary date than by Daniel's future. When she
could not gather anything past her three facts,
she determined that Daniel had to go public: On
Theodora's show, fittingly, he would announce

the truth and they would see what happened next. The reporters of the world loved this family; they would always and forever be on a Ransom team; let them chew on this.

Daniel was accustomed to turmoil. But if this failed, living with her would be hell on earth.

Though Michael Thiell had a difficult bride, he was going to have a terrific mother-in-law. Venice's mother was a doll. Wait until he, Daniel, got married. His wife would have Catherine Ransom for a mother-in-law. There'd probably be a second murder.

Daniel struggled to give his mother what she required, but he also struggled to keep a distance between them. Coming home with a girl caused lots of distance. There was no end to the girls willing to come. Daniel's fame, as exhausting as his mother, lined them up. Invariably the girls told him what they had been doing at the moment his father was shot. Then they would tell him how adorable he had been in his little black suit, walking his mother into the cathedral.

Daniel had not cried since the day he was immortalized on film as the little boy who wept for Daddy. But he was forced to see himself, relentlessly exposed year in and year out, whenever the clips were rerun.

If he had thought about it — how the world

had tuned in to his childhood; trespassed on him every mile and classroom of the way; observed his torn jeans and baseball strikeouts, his honors in biology and his failures on stage, his braces and his latest sailboat — he would have gone insane.

He had dreaded the event held in the Egyptian Room. In all four years of their friendship, he had not met Michael's father and was not the least interested in J Thiell's pet charities. They had been invited solely for the Ransom name.

His mother was in one of her worst moods. When at the last minute she had a migraine, she expected Daniel to stay home with her. Suddenly the Egyptian Room became a sanctuary, where he could be *away* from his mother. "One of us has to go," he had said lightly. "I'll tell you all about it."

Well . . . he would tell her nothing.

Because at the edge of the reflecting pool, he had actually met a girl he would have brought home for the pleasure of her company. Annabel. A romantic name, and not the kind Daniel would have expected to like. Too decorative for his taste. And Annabel was decorative, but unlike other beautiful girls with whom he had been paired, she was serene. There was a calm to Annabel, as if the world were a companionable place for her, and whatever upsets she might be dealt, she would go on being comfortable and easy.

It was rare for Daniel to be easy with strangers. He had a public persona he slipped over his personality like a Halloween costume, keeping it between himself and the stranger. But Annabel had not recognized him. He did not have to listen while she went on and on about where she'd been when the senator was murdered. He did not have to nod, Yes, I am that Daniel Ransom, Yes, the senator was my father, Yes, it was very sad, Yes, I'm fascinated that you were in gymnastics, on the balance beam at the moment my father was shot.

Instead Daniel could share cake icing, which they both liked better than cake. Wonder how on earth the braiding of her hair and the interweaving of the gold cords had been accomplished. Stare at the thin white gauze of her Egyptian costume, which seemed transparent, and yet could not be seen through. Wonder, if he could see through it, what he would see.

I've known Annabel for three hours, he thought, and I am in deeper than I've ever been with a girl.

What would happen when he introduced himself? Would she demand an autograph, beg to be photographed with him, get all giggly and silly? Would he despise her?

He helped Annabel into the taxi. The combination of her smile, her voice, and her scent made him dizzy.

I think, thought Daniel Madison Ransom, that this is called falling in love.

FOUR

"How was the Egyptian Room?" said Hollings Jayquith, bending over to kiss his daughter. He was a hard lean athlete, always in a dark and serious suit unless he was on a ball court, in which case he played in a dark and serious manner. Everything about him was long and thin, all his edges were sharp, all his speech quick.

Annabel was snuggled up in front of the television. At Wythefield, television had been impossible to come by. You had to go to the student center, since TVs were not allowed in the rooms, and in all four years, Annabel had failed to get to the television first. Invariably somebody was already tuned to a show she didn't want to see. Besides, what with required sports, formal dinners, and enforced study hours from seven to ten, there was not much TV time.

Now, Wythefield graduate that she was, Annabel could have supper while watching *Jeopardy* and *Star Trek*.

Her father eyed the screen in disgust. Hollings Jayquith felt that television — even Aunt Theodora — was a great waste of precious time. "For this I shipped you away for four years and suffered in a lonely house?" he said. He caught her loose hair and ponytailed it vertically, like Woody Woodpecker. "For this I underwrote the costs of an entire boarding school and gave them a new library? So you could watch reruns?"

"Daddy." She tilted way back and they regarded each other upside down. "You did not give them a new library."

"Okay, a new encyclopedia."

They laughed.

"Yes. For this," said Annabel. She patted the sofa. It was so nice to have her father home. She was, however, slightly suspicious. Hollings Jayquith did not banter. This easygoing conversation was out of character. "Sit down and watch *Jeopardy* with me. I'm rooting for the guy on the left, Daddy. Isn't he cute?"

"He looks dorky to me." Her father took great interest in the boys Annabel liked. Without exception he considered them dorks and was quick to point out their flaws and shortcomings.

"He's very dorky," admitted Annabel, "but he's still cute."

Her father folded his arms. It was not a good sign. The sharper his elbows, the worse his mood. She had a feeling the teasing was over. Sure enough, in a taut voice, her father said, "Tell me about the Egyptian Room, Annabel."

The Bruce-Newcombes had told. Well, she had known they would. Eighteen, and she was as supervised as most ten-year-olds. Boarding school required passes and permissions and sign-ins to go anywhere with anybody, and home was no different. "I met somebody there," she said carefully, "and we went on to a club he belongs to." She had phoned the museum so the Bruce-Newcombes wouldn't worry. And they told anyway. That's the last time I admire her nasty old pearls and diamonds, she thought.

"Who was this boy?" Her father's voice incised the air like a glass cutter.

Annabel, who left the verbal fights to her Aunt Theodora, felt a fight coming on. She should be bouncing in her corner of the ring, jabbing the air, not curled like a kitten under the comforter. "Man, not boy," Annabel corrected her father. "He's twenty-two. He's going to law school in September."

"What's his name?" demanded Hollings.

She did not want her father to possess Daniel's name. She did not want to hear him say (as he had of Gavin), "Doesn't have his family's brains, does he?" She did not want him to say (as he had of Jeremy), "Kind of low-slung, isn't he? Reminds me of an ape."

Last night had been precious. Short, far too short: a single evening. But long on feeling. Through Daniel's wonderful smile, Annabel could see into his heart. It was a generous heart, full of duty toward his family. A heart that accepted the demands of a Ransom's life. A strong heart.

In her own heart, she kept him a secret, but he was there. She loved having him unknown except to her. She wasn't even telephoning Emmie to give her the details, as she had with every other boy she'd dated at Wythefield.

Besides, Daniel didn't know *her* last name. The right order was for Daniel to know first.

Her father had come first in every event in her life. She was aware of a great shift, as if Daniel, in the *Jeopardy* game of life, had acquired vastly more points, and was going to win. Her father was not first. Daniel, whom she had known only one night, came in ahead of him. Annabel shivered slightly, trying to see into the future.

Hollings Jayquith found the remote and shut off the television. Annabel was not eager to look up. Hollings Jayquith, angry, frightened even his daughter. The indulgent blue eyes could turn to glaciers and freeze the blood. "Annabel," said her father, "what was his name?"

"Daniel," she said. She could not remember a time when she had been purposely obstructive.

"Daniel *who*?"

"I didn't ask." This was true. She hadn't needed to ask.

"Annabel! I cannot believe this! You went alone into the city, late at night, with a man whose last name you don't even know?"

"Don't make it sound like a list of crimes, Daddy. We had a wonderful time. And he's not a dork. I promise. He's perfect."

"Nameless, but perfect?" said her father. He was soft-spoken with his anger. He never yelled. Never raised his voice. She forced herself to meet his eyes and knew immediately that he thought a lot more had happened than was the case. Nothing happened, Daddy, she thought. No sex, if that's what you're worried about. We laughed, Daddy. We understood each other, we were special to each other.

But if she said this, he would roll his eyes at the distant ceiling, he would turn his face away, as if another more sensible person were there listening. He would know better. He would make her feel like a little girl.

So she said nothing. I have not had many secrets in my life, she thought. There are no secrets in a girls' dorm anyway. But now I have one. *Daniel.*

Staying silent when her father wanted talk gave her power. No wonder Aunt Theodora likes this! thought Annabel. Being powerful is more fun than being beautiful.

"This is New York!" said her father. He was furious. "Muggings, murder, and kidnap are around the next corner."

"They are not! How many people do you actually know who get kidnapped? Not one! This isn't Beirut or Brazil! Don't say anything bad about New York. I love New York." *And I love Daniel Madison Ransom, who is my kind of New Yorker.*

She had expected this to be the summer of Venice's wedding. A summer filled with frothy dresses and frilly themes for parties: roses and lace and swans carved in ice. A summer of giggling with Emmie and dancing with strangers. Perhaps instead, this would be the summer she truly turned eighteen, and became a woman who made decisions, instead of her father's little girl. It amazed Annabel that she had been content with the way things were: that until this minute, this argument, she had accepted the way Theodora, Hollings, and Mrs. Donovan, the housekeeper, controlled her existence. No more, she thought, and new heady perfumes filled her: the scent of being in charge of her own life. She found herself smiling, and tried not to, since it would only anger her father more.

"We are leaving for the country this afternoon instead of Thursday," snapped her father. "I want no discussion on the topic."

Annabel didn't, either. Being sent to the country was no punishment. Daniel's Camp couldn't be twenty miles away. "All right," she said agreeably. Once when she'd had a crush on a local boy in the landscaping crew, she had referred to the Jayquith estate as "the country." All New Yorkers referred to their New England or Long Island weekend places as "the country." Her father even called the highway to get there "the country." How the boy had laughed. You see any crops? he had said. You see any cows? This isn't the country. This is just a Manhattan town house stuck in a field.

Annabel had wanted to go out with this boy. Jimmy, his name was. Aunt Theodora put a stop to it. We're looking for better things, she said firmly.

Things, thought Annabel. Now even more she did not want to tell her father that she had met Daniel Madison Ransom, because no "thing" would impress them more. How they would congratulate her, for finding "a better thing."

Her father, knowing he had made no dent in her thinking, regrouped. Annabel always thought of her father that way: in the plural: a man who was his own army division. "Sweetheart, you can't do things like that. No matter how attractive a man is. Maybe especially if he's attractive. You have to exercise great caution. You more than any girl! There are a lot of men out there who would cozy up to you for your money and your name."

Not this man, thought Annabel.

Her father knelt beside her. It was not his posture. He wanted so much to be eye level that he was willing to sink instead of having Annabel stand. "I have a world of enemies, Annabel. They can't hurt me, but they could take it out on you. Somebody who knows nothing but the gleam of gold from your necklace. A cokehead who'd as soon strangle you as look at you. That could be the man with whom you take that taxi. Promise me you will never go off with a stranger again."

She had misjudged him. He was not angry so much as terribly worried. Contrite, she opened her mouth to promise, or at least explain that Daniel Madison Ransom was a stranger to nobody, but her father did not wait. When Hollings Jayquith spoke, people obeyed, and he assumed his daughter would be among the obedient. Besides, he was too restless to stay any longer. He left, his hard shoes clattering on the marble floor, room after room, like pebbles scattered to leave a trail.

Her private phone rang before she could flick the TV on again.

Other than Emmie and a few other friends from Wythefield, people who needed to reach a Jayquith were given Hollings' office number. A pleasant voice requested the caller's name and number and announced that the Jayquiths, should they wish to return the call, would do so at their convenience.

Annabel had received one hate call in her life and that was enough. People were crazy out there, and jealous of wealth and fame. Giving clues about how to find you was against the rules. Last night had been a night for breaking rules, and she had broken that one easily. She had given Daniel both her phone numbers — Manhattan and Connecticut. And he had given his: Manhattan and Massachusetts. He didn't say The Camp for that second phone number and he didn't know that she knew.

She picked up the phone. Let it be Daniel. Not Emmie, wanting to talk wedding talk. Let it be

Daniel. She closed and rolled her lips, but not
for courage: for miming a kiss. "Hello?" She
even crossed her fingers. It had been a magical
night, after all, and maybe she should go on
trying magic. Annabel had tried to coax Daniel
to take her back to the museum to get the pennies
back. They were so powerful, she explained,
that I want to have them in my jewelry chest.
Daniel said no, because her wish would be destroyed. Whatever she had asked for might evaporate. So the Nile kept the pennies.

"Annabel? It's Daniel."

He had not evaporated. She laughed silently,
so happy to hear his voice she'd be laughing all
night. He had been fishing, Daniel told her. Fishing at his camp.

Some camp, thought Annabel. But she let him
get away with it. She loved having more knowledge, holding secrets in her heart.

They talked for hours. Annabel sprawled on
her back and then on the carpet. She did step
exercises on a needlepointed footstool. Then she
lay upside down, draping her feet over the sofa
back. Telephones were gifts of the gods.

"What are you doing the rest of the week?"
he asked.

"Getting ready for a wedding." Annabel made
a bet with herself when he would break in to

her description. "My best friend's sister's wedding. I'm one of ten bridesmaids. I'll blend in."

"You could never blend in," Daniel assured her.

"Venice was going to wear leather instead of a bridal gown and make the guests bungee jump instead of drink champagne, but — "

"There cannot be another bride named Venice!" cried Daniel. "I'm in the same wedding! I'm sure of it. I was at Harvard with Michael. I'm one of ten ushers!"

"You won't blend in, either," Annabel said softly.

She could feel the emotion between them, remembering each other's textures and scents and sounds. Who is he remembering? she thought. Nefertiti? Cleopatra? There was no Annabel there. What if he meets the real me and he's disappointed? She shivered, suddenly afraid, suddenly counting on Venice's wedding as she had never counted on anything.

"So," said Daniel finally.

"So I'll see you at the rehearsal," she said. Her throat was tight. She had not been nervous through the entire phone call and now she was sick with fear that something could go wrong. That the penny wish would evaporate after all, and she would be lonely forever.

"I'll miss the rehearsal," said Daniel. "I . . .
uh . . . have a project. But I'll see you at the
wedding."

Miss the rehearsal! But it was going to be a
wonderful party! Twenty college kids, a wild
silly all-nighter, perfect for a second date. Could
Annabel risk suggesting they walk down the
aisle together? She said, "It'll be a long week,
waiting." That was risky, too, hinting he should
ask her out before the weekend. Would he be
threatened?

"If we could get together before then, I would.
But this — endeavor — is — keeping me involved."

He didn't know her well enough to tell her
what his project was. But he would! They would
do it together, whatever it was.

Daniel said, "In another week or so I'll be
free." He paused. "Will you?"

She threw back her head in silent joyful laughter. "Yes."

Jade was the only person under sixty. The
white- and gray-haired ladies (all the men, they
told her, had died) thought she was adorable.
"Doesn't she look like that reporter?" they said
to each other. "What's-her-name? The one who
does the specials."

"Theodora Jayquith!" the rest cried. "Exactly like her!"

"Did you know," said one, "that Theodora's brother Hollings has a magnificent estate in Litchfield?" They spoke as if they knew the Jayquith family, and in a way they did. Anybody who read checkout counter magazines and newspapers was up-to-date on the Jayquiths.

"Have you been there?" asked Jade.

"Goodness me, no! Nobody can go there. It's enclosed. Guards. Attack dogs. Barbed wire. But we drive past the entrance and I'll point it out. Hollings Jayquith would be a catch, wouldn't he, girls?" said the girl who had to be seventy-five. "Wife died years ago," she confided to Jade. "He never remarried. All that money, just waiting to be spent."

On me, thought Jade. On a niece, not a second wife.

The scenery was lovely — hills, villages, black-shuttered white-painted colonials. The girls played bridge as if still in each other's living rooms. "Millionaires live in those," said the "girls," pointing out the bus windows. "The richer you are, the more likely you'll own a country house up here. Nice drive from the city. Litchfield has 'em all: millionaires, billionaires, producers, stars. Must drive the locals crazy, all those demanding New Yorkers who show up for a weekend now and then to play tennis and sniff the mountain air, give parties and go home."

It sounded perfect to Jade, who could not imagine wanting to sniff mountain air when the atmosphere at home was the Jayquith.

Eleven Levels Road turned right off the main road. It must have had twenty levels. Probably whoever named it got sick of counting the bumps and rises. "There's the drive!" crowed her friend.

Jade would have missed it. A woods of evergreens — hollies and hemlocks and pine — backed against a remarkably high stone wall. Deep in the greenery was a black iron gate, flanked by stone pillars. As the bus groaned by, trying to get up to the eleventh level, Jade saw electronic gear fastened to the gate.

Her fantasies ground to a halt.

Nobody would swing those gates open for her.

Sweaty and dusty in her Ohio clothes, she would be forced to plead by wire. "I'm Theodora's daughter, please let me in."

The only difference from New York City would be that the police would take longer to arrive, having to cover such a distance.

FIVE

Annabel and Emmie were being nasty, placing bets on how long the marriage would last. "I give it two years," said Annabel.

Emmie hooted. "Six weeks," she said firmly. "Remember this is my sister that poor old Michael is marrying. How long could anybody live with her?"

The two girls were in the second limousine, headed to the church. Venice's family had of course supplied the rest of the limousines, but Annabel's father had insisted she must go in her own.

Annabel felt as if her skin had blistered. Sunburned from love, she thought. She could not wait to see Daniel. Every word he had spoken replayed like a cherished cassette in her mind.

If only she were wearing something romantic. Any other wedding in the world, and she'd be sweet and frothy, her gown long and delicate. Not Venice's. Venice had chosen black and white for the bridal party, every bridesmaid slightly different, so when the girls lined up, they presented a violent zigzag slash across the front of the church.

When I marry, thought Annabel, I'll choose colors to celebrate by. Colors to send up fireworks by. My colors will be the colors of hearts beating faster and pulses racing.

Annabel cupped her long thin fingers over her face, hiding her wild excitement and pleasure behind her own hands. How it magnified love to keep it instead of share it! She, Annabel, to whose room every Wythefield girl had come to hear the best gossip, had managed to keep a secret.

Emmie dug her elbow into Annabel. "Well?"

Annabel hauled herself back to the topic. Daniel leaned dark and perfect against the wall of her mind. She felt out of breath. "Six weeks with Venice would knock the stuffing out of anybody," she agreed.

Emmie, of course, had brought reading material, because even at her own sister's wedding, Emmie wasn't going to risk being without something to read. She leafed through *Famous*, noting that Prince Andrew had visited the Serengeti and Madonna had written a book.

Annabel wanted a television career like her aunt's. She loved the excitement; meeting important people, traveling to exotic places. She loved to visit the twelfth floor of the Jayquith Building, from which Theodora's thirty minutes were broadcast. Aunt Theodora said it was going to be tricky — Annabel as a TV reporter. "You're too lovely," said her aunt. "I'm handsome. It's good for women in journalism to be handsome. But you are ethereal. It doesn't inspire people to believe in you. The other problem is your name. There *cannot* be another Jayquith in television journalism."

Theodora was matter-of-fact about this. *She* was the Jayquith. She was *the* Jayquith. Even for her beloved niece, there would be no sharing that last name. "You'll have to change your name or get married," said Theodora, "and use his last name."

I'll just have to get married, thought Annabel, shivering with her own heat. Annabel Ransom. I like it. Two against fame is better than one. With Daniel, fame might even be fun.

"Look at this!" cried Emmie, waving *Famous* in Annabel's face.

Annabel glanced over.

The first photo was so poor Annabel didn't recognize her own father. The media were not invited to her father's events. Hollings Jayquith kept fame at bay with tinted windows and private jets, high fences and security guards, but mostly he kept fame at bay with silence.

The photo was grainy and had been taken from a distance by a photographer who had been kicked off the site. Readers of *Famous* would not recognize the subject if they ran into him on the street. But that was not a problem, because Hollings Jayquith was never on the street.

The second was a rerun of their famous birthday party photo of Annabel. They'd have loved an Egyptian night picture, she thought.

"Read it," commanded Emmie.

Even movie stars and rock singers are not as fascinating to the American public as the very rich, and Hollings Jayquith is among the richest of all. His wealth is awesome. Impossible to measure, it spans the globe. His parties, given on his yacht or his own ballroom in his own New York hotel, are the stuff of legend. He is known for astoundingly large donations to charity.

His wife, Eleanor, died years ago. Last winter, his daughter, Annabel, had America's most splendiferous eighteenth birthday party. Like Princess Caroline of Monaco and Princess Diana of England,

Annabel Jayquith was born to this life.
So far, Annabel has done nothing except
go to school and be beautiful. Where are
the scandals and wild behavior we expect
in our princesses? Does Hollings Jayquith keep her escapades out of the news?
He certainly has the clout. Come on,
Annabel, stop being somebody's daughter or somebody's niece! Show us yourself. We want action!

Annabel had to laugh. "I've been telling
Daddy for years that what our family needs is a
really good scandal. How shall I begin?"

Emmie was full of scandalous ideas. The first
was that just before Venice and Michael said their
vows, Annabel should change places with the
bride. What had Venice ever done to deserve
Michael Thiell, anyway? This would save Venice
and Michael from getting divorced later and
would actually be an act of decency.

"Stop this!" said Tommy. The chauffeur had
driven Annabel's father for years and listened to
a lot of conversations. This one was too much.
"First you place bets on the marriage when we
haven't even arrived at the church. Now you
want a different bride for Michael. You two are
sick and perverted."

A wonderful scandal, Annabel thought,

would be for Daniel and me to step up to the altar when Michael and Venice are done, and tell the minister we want to say *I do*, too.

"It'll be a messy divorce," warned Emmie. "Can't you just imagine my sister, Venice, versus Michael's father, J Thiell?"

"Why not Venice versus Michael?" Annabel wanted to know.

"Michael loves her. He'd give in. J Thiell never gave in to anybody in his life. Mr. Thiell's rather disgusting, really. I don't believe I'd want to celebrate Christmas and Thanksgiving with him. Venice likes to take on things like that, though. It will be a very exciting divorce," said Emmie. "I hope I'm not off at college when it comes."

"Stop it!" said Tommy. "You ghoul!"

"Oh, good," said Annabel. "At least we've scandalized somebody." She smiled at the chauffeur. He was a fixture in her life, as comforting as mail in the morning or hot water in the shower.

She forgot Tommy and Emmie. She stared at the dark limousine window, not seeing through it, a mist of diamond-dusted love between herself and the world. Daniel had become all weather, all events, all places, all people.

After a week of waiting, a week that had felt

like generations, she was going to be with him.
Only a minute now.

The limousine slowly halted at the church
steps.

Only seconds.

The seven limousines were black, their windows shadowed. Slowly, in complete possession
of the roads, they drew up in front of a stone
church with sharp-peaked Gothic windows.

Traffic stopped. Heads turned. Tourists
paused.

On the opposite side of the manicured New
England village green, a boy in an ordinary car
drew a deep breath and straightened his tie. This
was it. In spite of the heat, he shivered slightly.

A bride, wearing the most unbridelike gown
that the boy had ever seen, emerged from the
first limousine. Stiff swoops of white damask
arched around her shoulders as if she herself were
a Gothic window. She was more sculpture than
girl. Her hair was not just blonde, but truly
golden, and on her head she wore a crown of
flowers.

A stout father, traditional in striped trousers,
ascot, and long tails, took his daughter's arm.
He would be Mr. Pearse.

Video cameras recorded it. Photographers

knelt and circled, getting every angle. Wedding guests smiled gently. Out of the second and third limousines poured bridesmaids in black.

The boy had recently come from a funeral and for him black meant death.

He had thought bridesmaids should wear bright happy colors, shiny taffeta and dyed-to-match slippers. Not these girls. Harsh vertical shafts of black with asymmetrical slashes and shoulders.

He got out of his car, closing the door carefully. His breath was coming in short spurts. His hands were cold. He forced himself to walk casually, imitating the pace of the wedding guests: a languid, attention-getting, liquid walk.

You are not committing a crime, he said to himself. Not yet, anyway. They're the ones who commit crimes. You are only crashing a wedding. The worst that can happen is that you'll be refused entrance.

Even then, they wouldn't recognize his name. And his face? No recognition there, either. He bore no resemblance to his brother. He was safe. He thought of his brother, also safe. Safe in the grave.

The lot filled with more limousines, Mercedes, lovely old Rolls Royces, and a multitude of tiny European sports cars shaped like triangles shooting for the moon. The people who got out were, like the bride, dressed to stun the world.

The boy was wearing his best suit. In spite of that, he was the least well-dressed person at the wedding. He reminded himself of his name. He was Alex. He mustn't forget it. Alex.

The bridesmaids, giggling, waved at their friends, hugged each other, and posed for informal photographs.

He was amazed by the number of photographers present. This was no team preparing the wedding album. These were reporters. He slid behind a thickly blossoming purple rhododendron to prevent being caught forever in a reporter's camera. Pretending that he, too, had friends to whom he must wave, the boy shielded his face and slipped quietly into the church.

It was dim, the bright sunlight filtered by stained glass. Wine-red carpet covered the aisles. Narrow pews were filling with beautiful people. He recognized a rock star for whose autograph he would have given his car. He recognized a former President of the United States. A Wall Street stockbroker fresh out of prison after multimillion dollar swindles.

An usher, his tailed jacket sweetly traditional against the drama of the bridesmaids, smiled in welcome. The usher was broad shouldered: football-team wide, no padding beneath his jacket.

He seemed too energetic for the job of seating people: a repressed energy trembled beneath the black jacket and tails. The usher was —

Daniel Madison Ransom.

Alex was awestruck.

Who could forget the assassination of Senator Ransom? When had that been? A decade ago, maybe. But they were always replaying the murder on television. Senator Ransom, instead of changing America, left a weeping wife, a little son, and a shocked nation.

"Friend of the bride or groom?" whispered Daniel, actually speaking to the boy.

In a weird way, Alex felt as if they were buddies, had been to school together or something. He knew a thousand things about Daniel, but Daniel neither knew nor cared to know a single thing about him. How did Daniel feel about that? Or did the rich and famous simply take it in stride, forgetting or never knowing that public curiosity existed? "Bride," said the boy softly, since he was certainly no friend of the groom.

The boy was escorted to a pew in which three other guests had already been seated. A married couple, incredibly handsome in their fifties, and with them — he caught his breath — Theodora Jayquith.

How astonishing that Daniel Madison Ransom — who would *never* have given the woman

an interview — had been the one to seat her!
They had to have recognized each other. Did
Theodora regard Daniel as a challenge? As prey?
Did she plan to net him at the reception, and
plant him firmly in front of her own cameras?
Her trophy?

And Daniel? Had he any knowledge of who
really killed his father? He couldn't have. He
would not be at this wedding if he did.

The boy pretended not to recognize Theodora
Jayquith. He pretended, when they smiled
slightly, as people sitting crushed against each
other must, that he never watched television
news and had no earthly idea who she might be.

The next time he saw her show, would his
own face be on it?

Because he intended to make news.

The worst kind of news.

Here — to this church — would come the
person he wanted to kill.

It was good that Emmie was slender. Black
layers and silvery white capelets cascaded over
her shoulders and plunged down her sides, an-
gling around her ankles. Venice had chosen
gowns that were demanding on the eye, and
required beauty. Emmie was not beautiful. She
had finally ceased to be jealous of Annabel's
beauty, although being her roommate had placed

Emmie forever in second position. But she was still jealous of how Annabel attracted men. Being unloved had hurt Emmie in boarding school, but boarding school was a rehearsal. This summer counted.

Emmie had her heart set on finding a boyfriend at the wedding.

Michael, of course, was taken, although in Emmie's opinion, only temporarily. Venice was a very difficult person. There were also ten ushers. According to Michael, two were engaged and two heavily involved. That left six.

But they will not, she thought, a terrible resigned sadness filling her heart, choose me. They'll choose Annabel. Or Candice.

Emmie saw the years passing by, as she ceased to be a plain freckled girl and became a thick freckled matron. Venice would get divorced, and have affairs, and more marriages, because that was the kind of girl she was. But where would Emmie be? On the sidelines. Emmie was brilliant in math and had long ago decided to be an engineer. Emmie knew she could hold her own in college. She expected to be pretty impressive. But sometimes being impressive lost its appeal.

Sometimes — on her sister's wedding day, for example — she just wanted to be loved.

I have enough money, she thought. They could marry me for that. Perhaps I should advertise. *WANTED: handsome stud who needs cash.*

The limousine stopped. Emmie gathered her black and white panels carefully.

She smiled routinely at a handsome young man who was crossing the village street. Definitely a wedding guest. When else does a young man wear a black jacket with satin lapels? His smile back was quick with interest. He adjusted his scarlet bow tie, as if he worried about her opinion.

Behind him cascaded the green lace of willow trees. Dozens of laughing people of every age poured out of cars and cried greetings across the church lawn. Church bells rang. Even Venice, moving with care, keeping her gown off the grass, seemed soft and warm, displaying possibilities that until now only Michael had seen. The bridesmaids gathered, their dramatic gowns made serene by the green grass and the blue sky.

The romance that had eluded Emmie throughout planning the wedding suddenly touched her heart. She wanted the wedding to be beautiful, and the marriage to last forever.

She waved at the boy. He waved back, smiling shyly.

Maybe it's him! Emmie told herself, full of hope.

The intensity of falling in love left nothing between Daniel and his emotions. He was peeled like an orange.

Michael had known right away that something had happened. He and Daniel talked the day after the Egyptian Wing dance, and Michael said, "So what's going on?"

"I had a nice weekend," was all Daniel could manage.

Michael laughed softly. Their friendship did not require details.

Daniel actually counted the hours until he saw Annabel again, the way when he was a kid at boarding school he used to count the hours until finals were over and he could go home to a room and a shower of his own. At the wedding he and Annabel would dance again, and kiss, and begin the scary, beautiful process of finding out about each other. Finding out, he thought, laughing, what she looks like without a ton of Nefertiti makeup.

Between seating guests, Daniel kept going back to the arched open doors, watching for the arrival of the bridesmaids. He was there when her limousine stopped, when some other lucky man helped her out.

He hardly knew her.

She was intoxicatingly beautiful. Clouds of soft black hair lay on her shoulders like a gathering storm. Her ethereal features seemed to float in happiness. He had know she would be lovely out of the Egyptian costume, but he had not known she would be this lovely.

Behind her the blossoming trees were a stage set. He felt connected to Annabel by every invisible wave: radio wave and light wave and ultraviolet wave. The world blurred at the edges. Daniel did not notice the strange black and white gown. He saw only the girl within it.

He left his duties and threaded his way through the press of people. His heart beat as if he had just finished rowing for the Harvard team. Venice's little sister came running up to introduce him. He managed to remember Emmie's name.

Annabel's smile tumbled toward Daniel. He could have caught it, like a thrown bouquet.

"Annabel Jayquith," said Emmie Pearse.

Litchfield was beautiful, if you liked grass and white buildings.

Jade did not.

"Oooooh!" squealed her gray-haired ladies. "A wedding! Ooooooh, look at the beautiful bride!"

Jade did not. Only her own future mattered to Jade. One plan after another slotted into her mind, and had to be discarded. She had so little time. She must use it well.

"Ooooooh! Look!" cried the bridge players, overcome. "Check out the wedding guests! There's Theodora Jayquith! Right there!"

Jade looked.

"Annabel darling!" cried Venice's mother, hugging her several times. "Why isn't your father here? What has happened to the man? I'm beside myself. You know I adore Hollings."

Annabel shook her head in apology. "Business, Mrs. Pearse. I'm mad at him myself. He ought to be able to arrange his life better, don't you think?"

"Oh, yes, but I think that about all men."

The groomsmen gathered at the top of the church steps. It was time to line up.

Daniel, edging through the crowd, was momentarily sideways to her, his profile as demanding as his personality. For a heartbeat, she treasured Daniel privately, as if he were a portrait on her wall, for her eyes only.

Mrs. Pearse repeated her views on men. A lifetime of social training prevented Annabel from shoving Mrs. Pearse to the grass and running right over her body to reach Daniel. The wedding consultant passed out the bouquets. Annabel took hers without looking.

Emmie was performing introductions.

Candice, another bridesmaid, burbled all over Daniel. "What a pleasure! Of course I would have recognized you anywhere. You know what? When your father was killed, I was taking a quiz about the Revolutionary War. I kept the pencil."

Daniel smiled courteously in Candice's direction, but his eyes, seeking Annabel, went through her. Yes! thought Annabel, I want your eyes to go all the way through, I want you to know me that well.

Annabel let Emmie introduce her. Daniel's wonderful grin was emerging. His eyebrows met in the middle and became a single. She would get to know those two eyebrows.

"And this," said Emmie, "is Annabel . . ."

Their fingertips touched. They jumped, as if from static shock. They were on fire for each other.

". . . Jayquith," said Emmie.

"Jayquith?" Daniel froze. His smile faded. His hand withered. Daniel actually looked down at Annabel's hand, and stepped back, as if to avoid contamination.

Candice, Gavin, Bruce, Amanda, Spencer —

all turned, gaping, mentally photographing what was happening.

"Daniel?" said Annabel. The stares of the rest of the bridal party were knives. "What — ?"

The expression on Daniel's face had changed from desire to loathing. He actually dusted his hands off, as if removing her. "I didn't know," he said. His voice shook. "You should have told me. Did you plan this? Did your father order you to get to know me?"

Annabel could not see Daniel clearly anymore: Shock blurred him. Know what? she thought. She felt Candice's fascination, heard Gavin catch his breath, half-saw Emmie freeze.

"I will not stand in public next to a Jayquith." He did not say her last name as much as spit it. Then he turned away without missing another beat. Changed places with Gavin. Struck up a bright conversation with Candice, his new partner.

The wedding consultant, greedy with delight to have been a witness to this scene, pushed everybody inside the church.

Annabel had gripped her bouquet so tightly all the stems were snapped.

A photographer — not the one Venice had hired for the wedding pictures, but a professional follower of the famous — shoved his camera into her face. He snapped over and over and over again, immortalizing her single tear, her white-knuckled fingers, her broken bouquet. A huge grin split his face: He was happy. He could sell these.

My name, she thought. I'm as doomed as Venice's marriage. By my own name.

SIX
___

When people hurt you, Hollings Jayquith liked to say, never let it show. Think of yourself as a baseball that you refuse to throw. You could, of course. You could throw yourself a hundred miles an hour and smash faces and windows. But you won't. You'll stitch yourself down. Never never never let them see how deeply they have cut you.

Annabel tried to stitch herself down. But she had never been cut so deeply and the stitching did not hold. I'm going to come apart in this church, in front of all these people, among a score of photographers and my aunt who has never fallen apart for anything or anybody on earth.

Three trumpeters stood on the chancel steps, their graceful instruments gleaming like beaten gold. What primitive emotions a trumpet call arouses. The guests shivered, as if armies were on the march, or danger.

I am eighteen, she told herself. I am poised, sophisticated. I will get through the rest of this afternoon and evening. I will not flinch, I will not cry. I will neither flush nor stumble. I will not let Daniel see how deeply he has hurt me.

Annabel cast a glance behind her. Venice was ready. The tall cowl of her gown was like a white sunrise behind her hair. She actually looked like the girl Michael thought he was marrying. All the bridesmaids had been given gold necklaces hung with tiny gold treble clefs, a bright speck of diamond glittering from the curl of each clef. Pure Michael, if he thought his marriage to Venice would be gold.

Poor me, thought Annabel. *I am gold.*

The bridesmaids came in from the west and the groomsmen from the east. Annabel, seventh in line, emerged from the anteroom just as Daniel offered his arm to Candice. Candice, puffed with importance, swung them toward the photographers, to be immortalized with Daniel Madison Ransom. Daniel's eyes — the same eyes that had looked so deep — slid up and over Annabel, as if she were stairs or carpet.

The photographer who'd gotten her tear leaped into the aisle between them, kneeling, springing up and about like a Russian dancer, clicking insanely at her face. Annabel felt as if she'were in an asylum, not a church.

I will not cry. I have been trained in front of the public eye. I will not give that photographer a second shot into my soul.

Gavin emerged where Daniel had been a moment earlier. The wedding consultant gave Annabel a gentle push in the small of her back and she forced herself to glide toward Gavin. "Gavin," she murmured, summoning a smile, "you look so handsome." Gavin was nice. She had known him all her life. Boring, solid, steady. Rich of course. Destined for a comfortable life. But he was only Gavin. He would never be more.

He was one thing, though: He was kind. He did not refer to Daniel's flinging of verbal stones. Instead he kissed her hot cheek, a kiss of comfort and friendship. Of course the photographer did not bother to get that; who cared about Gavin's kiss when you could have Daniel's slap?

Would it be better to be married to Gavin, who was dull but kind, than to Daniel, who was exciting but cruel?

Annabel and Gavin moved slowly. It was torture. She smiled at the guests. She knew fewer than she had expected. but exposure to stares hurt more than she had expected. Emmie and I daydreamed about this wedding for weeks and weeks, she thought, and it's hell, not heaven.

Daniel was ten paces ahead. The hair she had never touched, the shoulders she had never caressed, the reasons she did not know.

Annabel did not have a temper and she would not explode. She expected that someday, instead, she would *im*plode. She would be a building detonated by experts. She would cave in. There would be nothing left of Annabel Jayquith but dust and rubble.

If a biography were written of her, each page would have two columns. In the public column, would be her out-loud remarks: Lovely day for a wedding, so nice to see you, Mrs. Pearse, what perfect flowers! The private column would give readers access to her heart. No sentences. Just cries of pain. *Mama! Daddy! Daniel! Please! Not this!*

So much pain. Perhaps people lived like this, their hearts carved away, while their lungs went on and their legs continued to move. They were bridesmaids in weddings and tennis partners over the summer and went on to college. And their first loves dissolved like pearls in acid.

Aunt Theodora had frosted her hair even lighter. The earrings today were great strips of foil. They might have been peeled off a chrome bumper. She looked stunning and overly dramatic, as if it were her wedding. What have you done to Daniel, thought Annabel, that he won't stand next to me because of our name?

It took all her control not to stop at Theodora's pew and shriek at her. I have gone to so many dumb mixers, thought Annabel, and ridiculous parties and annoying get-togethers. And to meet what? Skinny, mindless, boozing dorks who love me for my last name. Then I meet *him*. And he *hates* me for my last name! Oh, Aunt Theodora, I hate you right back! How could you do this to me? What interview was it? What fact did you uncover, what unbearable pressure did you apply, to make Daniel feel this way?

She had to distract herself with something. Names, she would think of names. Gavin-SpencerCandiceVeniceEmmieMichael. If she ever had a daughter, what kind of name would she pick? Trendy and televisiony like Tiffany? No frills like Jane? Inherited like Eleanor Hope? Weird like Venice?

It did not distract her. The only name she cared about was Daniel.

And the only name that will ever matter, she thought, is Jayquith.

Gavin patted her knotted fingers. "No big deal," he breathed. "I've been in six weddings. All we do is hang out at the altar." The ponderous hesitation step finally brought them to the chancel steps. She let go of Gavin's arm. The congregation was not looking at her. They had turned to see the bride. Even Theodora.

The close dark church was heavy with the scent of lilies of the valley. Even after all these years it reminded Annabel of her mother. Do you wish you were here, Mama? thought Annabel. Did you think about my wedding? About whether I would have true love and lilies of the valley banked along the window ledges of my church?

But what if I don't have a wedding? What if I have already met the only man I could love and he hates me? What if I don't get a second chance, and I have to take second best?

"I will," said Venice.

Annabel was amazed. Venice had actually promised to honor and cherish and love Michael above all others. Let it be! thought Annabel. Let her keep the promise. Let her marriage last.

"I will," said Michael, who had to brush his cheek dry.

"You may kiss the bride," said the rector, smiling gently.

The entire congregation was sniffling. Everyone who knew and loved Venice or Michael was weepy. Annabel did not risk it. If she began crying, she might never stop. She looked down the row of groomsmen, outlined in starched white collars and cuffs like old-fashioned black-and-white portraits. Daniel was looking up at

the ceiling, or at God, or just to keep his own
tears from overflowing.

*I want you, Daniel. And I am a Jayquith. We do
not give in. We get what we want.*

Crashing the wedding had been easy. Somehow Alex had eased his way into the church;
perhaps in country villages where you were supposed to have neighborly attitudes, the rector
didn't allow checking invitations. Perhaps nobody thought a stranger would try to get into a
church. The reception would be different.

Had it been Daniel Madison Ransom's wedding, there would have been circling helicopters,
drooling photographers, and hordes of panting
autograph seekers. Somebody must have leaked
the guest list, because the handful of photographers there were concentrating on Daniel and
Annabel.

Venice Pearse's family was only rich, not famous, and as for the Thiells, they kept a low
profile. People who own entire cities for gambling do not like to be recognized. It was confusing that J Thiell had recently asked for
publicity. J Thiell didn't care about green spaces.
The only green thing J Thiell cared about was
money.

The boy memorized the face of the photographer who had jammed his camera into the

Jayquith girl's face. He had to stay out of photographs.

Crashing the reception worried him. But at any wedding, half the wedding guests wouldn't know the other half. He could easily say, "I was in school with John," and who was to know who John was, or whether anybody had been in school with him? And he was the right age, or could pass for it. If anyone probed, he'd change the topic; he'd say, "Wasn't the bride lovely? Beautiful ceremony." If he could just get himself on the grounds of the bride's estate, he'd be fine.

Lying so much made him nervous. Interesting, thought Alex. Planning a murder doesn't bother me, but being an imposter does.

He had counted on cadging a ride from somebody at the church, but he had not counted on sitting next to Theodora Jayquith. Did he dare ask her for a lift? She had begun her spectacular career as an investigative reporter. What if she decided to do a little investigating about him? He slid away from Theodora and crowded next to the young people, laughing loudly when they did. He slapped somebody's back when somebody slapped his.

Flashbulbs went off. The boy flinched and ducked, but of course nobody wanted his picture. He felt like a jerk. The wedding photographers captured bride and groom, bride and father, bride and mother. They plucked at this person and shunted that person over and everybody was smiling so hard their cheeks trembled.

"So clever of you to have the wedding here in the country," gushed the older guests to Mrs. Pearse.

The country, thought the boy. As if country people had so many limousines to go around they don't have to hire any.

The bride's mother swarmed over the bridal party, hugging and bubbling, "Daniel, my dear," she cried, "such a pleasure to have you with us. Congratulations on doing so well at Harvard. And you and Michael will both be in law school in the fall! How exciting."

Daniel did not look excited. He looked as if he would prefer to hitchhike home than attend a wedding reception.

For a moment the boy considered changing his plans. I could talk to Daniel, he thought. But would he help, or would he stop me? His father and my brother, killed by the same man. I can half prove it. But not enough for court. Not enough for police. It's been ten years for Daniel. Maybe he's forgotten the murder of his father. It's been only six months since my brother was murdered. I have forgotten nothing. The law won't help me. I have to be my own law.

"On to the reception!" cried Mrs. Pearse. "Venice! Michael! Emmie! Annabel! Daniel! Gavin! Come on, now." She was a collie herding the wedding party, nipping at their heels. Alex memorized the names. Venice, Michael, Emmie, Annabel, Daniel, Gavin.

Limousines took the bridal party — in different order from their arrival; the groom instead of the father accompanied the bride. Sleek contemporary vans, with pointy-glassed front ends, slid up to the church steps to carry the house guests of the Pearses and Thiells.

Wiping sweaty hands on his trousers, Alex crowded into a cranberry-red van with eleven other passengers. He ended up holding a girl in his lap. Everybody was giggling, the way kids do when too many are crammed into too little space. During the five-mile drive to the reception, he evaded questions while making friends. Two of the boys actually mentioned tennis games later on; this seemed to be a very tennis-oriented crowd, and Venice's estate had several courts. The boy found himself agreeing to a match.

Either he had what it took to be an actor, or this was a particularly easily duped crowd.

Luck be a lady tonight, he thought. And thought of the girl who had smiled at him, the

sister of the bride. Emmie. She had a lonely look
to her.

She would be his luck.

Jayquith.

Daniel was so shocked that all the poise he'd
gathered in all the years of public life deserted
him.

The irony of it! To meet a girl he could love —
and she was a Jayquith. No wonder Daniel had
felt a core of strength in her. Look at her genes!

There was no greater louse on earth than Hollings Jayquith. You didn't amass that kind of
fortune without crawling beneath rocks. Hollings Jayquith had spent a lifetime smashing the
people in his way like a machine crushing soda
cans. He had smashed Senator Madison Ransom.
Hired it to be done, of course. Hollings never
did anything unpleasant himself.

Daniel made it through the ceremony without
looking at Annabel, and even through the pho-
tography session, although the photographer
moved him next to Annabel and they both
flinched. Her cheek stained as red as if it bore
his handprint from a slap.

I will not feel guilty! thought Daniel. This is
not my fault! Con artist!

He pulled out every trick he used to deal with
his mother, hiding some of himself, faking the

rest. It didn't work. Annabel remained, for Daniel, the beautiful girl of the beautiful hours in the Egyptian Wing.

I should have known. Who else is named Annabel? The Cleopatra hair and eyes threw me.

So, Annabel. Did Daddy skip the fund-raiser and send you instead? Your little mission to make friends with Daniel Madison Ransom? Your little nonsense with the pennies . . . as if a Jayquith needed wishes. Your father has connections the world over. He found out my father was on to him. It's no surprise that ten years later, he would also find out that my mother had begun to catch on.

Of course, it's my own fault for deciding to announce the truth on Theodora's show. I have to hurt them back somehow, don't I? What better way than to have the murderer named on his own sister's live television show — in front of tens of millions of people — and see what she says.

But of course there's nothing Theodora and Hollings don't share. She would call him, announce that she gets the first Ransom interview ever, just as she had all the Senator Ransom interviews. Hollings would realize we have evidence. He'd start to work. He has to squelch it. What better way than to have his lovely daughter appeal to my hormones?

"Thank you, Mrs. Pearse," said Daniel gravely. "Of course I'm very excited about law school." He hated the mere thought of law school. What was law but verbal confrontation? Physical fights, yes, that was fine with Daniel, he loved using his fists. Wrestling was his best sport. He would certainly have stayed with boxing if its dangers had not so terrified his mother. But speech? He did not want it. He did not want this entire afternoon. That photographer had gotten Annabel's tear. What an actress! Now he, Daniel, would be cast as the bad guy, making beautiful Annabel cry.

People were gawking. Guests were more interested in meeting Daniel Madison Ransom than in kissing the bride. Normally on these occasions he resorted to sunglasses, the wonderful blind wall behind which he could keep his eyes and his sanity. He hadn't brought them to the wedding. Too affected. It would be hours before he could cut out. Michael would never understand if Daniel skipped.

The Pearses' country place was a magnificent French manor, its white stucco walls shining in the sun and its turquoise-blue shutters reflecting the summer sky. Horses stood in high grass behind white fences and flowers splashed loudly in large patches.

Although the house had its own ballroom, and

could easily contain the largest wedding party, tented yellow pavilions had been erected on each side of the rose gardens, and filled with white chairs and round tables. Violinists and cellists were tuning. The sweet chaos of an orchestra getting ready filled the country air. Daniel heard the musical clink of crystal glasses, the laughter of friends.

Annabel was walking toward him.

Oh, no. No scenes, please. He had scenes too often with his mother. And what was he supposed to say to her? Hi, Annabel, I know we had a great time together, but your father murdered mine, and it's cut into my ardor.

No, Annabel, walk the other way, neither of us needs to do this, not with reporters skulking at the edge of the action and three hundred people eager for the next act.

Daniel's only hope was a waiter, balancing a tray of champagne glasses on his fingertips. If the waiter stood between them, maybe Daniel could avoid — but no. He could avoid nothing. From here on in, his whole life would be scenes and hurt.

He owed the truth to his father, to his mother, maybe even to America.

His mother was a difficult ally. To put it more factually, she was a mental case. Only a few hours ago, he had been planning on having An-

nabel as his ally. They'd be partners and get
through it together.

Right, he thought. A mixture of grief and re-
sentment and some other emotion he could not
identify swirled through him.

Love, he thought. That's the other emotion.
I really fell for her. Okay, Daniel, get tough, cut
the love out, don't give her an inch. This is Hollings Jayquith's daughter, don't ever forget it.

She's brave, I'll give her that. I wouldn't walk
up to a man that three hundred people are staring
at, knowing perfectly well I risk a second slap
in the face. But then, maybe she has an offer to
make. Maybe Daddy gave her a bargaining
position.

He wanted her to be innocent.

He wanted her to know nothing.

It came to him, when she was only a few steps
away, that he never wanted her to know. How
wonderful if this lovely girl could go on thinking
that her father was also wonderful. But she could
not. In only a few days, she would have more
knowledge of Hollings Jayquith than she de-
served.

A summer breeze lifted Annabel's soft hair,
as if it truly were a black cloud. He wanted to
hold the silkiness of it in his hands, against his
cheeks.

Stop it, stop it, Daniel ordered himself, but

nothing stopped. It was as if he had gotten on a roller coaster ride at an amusement park and he could not get off, no matter how much money and fame and training he had, until the ride ended.

"Champagne?" said the waiter, flourishing his silver tray. Daniel nodded and took one.

"No, thank you," said Annabel.

In the strange black-and-white bridesmaid gown, she seemed as much in costume as she had at the museum. He found himself wondering how she would look in a bathing suit or jeans. Terrific. She would definitely look terrific.

"There'll be toasts soon," the waiter reminded Annabel, moving the tray closer to her hand.

"No, thank you," she repeated courteously.

"Might as well take one," Daniel said. "You could just throw it at me."

She laughed slightly. "I may just do that," she said. Her voice was calm. Waiting for an explanation. She was willing to discuss this. He had met probably the only girl in America who really would understand his position . . . and he could never be seen with her again, let alone dance with her, or hold her close, or share his heart.

Emmie's heart had been breaking all day.

She could not talk to her mother. Daddy had discarded her several years before for a younger, lovelier woman who had her own L.A. clothing line. A trophy wife, people said. Your dad's earned a better one; why should he be stuck with the old one? Daddy had not done terribly well with trophy wife number one, and moved on to trophy wife number two. Then he started drinking too much, although this did not prevent him from acquiring trophy wife number three. Finally one day, he came home, and asked Emmie's mother if they could get back together.

Emmie's parents were polite, agreeing on most things and compromising on the rest. They did not seem like husband and wife. They were people renting a house together. They never had real conversation. Perhaps real conversation would hurt too much. Emmie did not want to go through what her mother had been through. She just wanted to be loved, for good and forever.

Emmie watched Annabel and Daniel, and Mr. Thiell dancing with his new daughter-in-law. Venice could be so peculiar. Mr. Thiell had said he would give her anything she wanted for her wedding gift. And did Venice ask for diamonds or emeralds, for a yacht or a fabulous car? No. She asked him to buy a parcel of land she had always admired and turn it into a wildlife preserve! It killed Emmie. Venice wasn't going to build a dream house there, or even pitch a tent. She wanted it fenced off forever, so that not even she could touch it.

Emmie wondered, if somebody offered her anything at all, anything on earth, what her answer would be.

"Hi," said someone cheerfully. It was the boy she'd seen when they got out of the limo. The shy one with the bright eyes and hesitant walk. "The wedding was breathtaking," he said. "You looked terrific. Is black fashionable at weddings? I thought you'd be in soft stuff, like roses or something."

Emmie loved how men were inarticulate about colors and styles. She said, "I voted for soft stuff. Cream and peach and lace. But Venice won, of course, because Venice always wins, so here we are looking like people who sleep on beds of nails."

The boy laughed. "The bridesmaids looked ready to take over a small country, actually. I'm Alex." He put out his hand.

"Emmie," she said. His hand was very warm. It was company. She wanted to keep it. "Sister of the bride. Are you a friend of Michael's?"

He shook his head. "Friend of John's. Did you go to Wythefield like the rest of the girls, Emmie?"

"Of course. We're Wythefield women from way back. Even my grandmother. Where did you go?"

"Harvard," he said.

"My neighbor Gilly goes there. Do you know Gilly?"

"I'd remember that name," he said. "No, I'm in college now. Where are you going in the fall, Emmie? Tell me about it. And do you mind if we start edging toward the food?"

Emmie walked with him toward the buffet. A boy as handsome as this would soon be swallowed up. Or he'd go off with John, whoever John was. Boys were loners. They were in groups only for a purpose, like sports or war. They didn't collect in knots, as girls did, to laugh and share and talk.

People enveloped them. "Emmie," they cried, "you look beautiful! What a dramatic gown! How like Venice to choose such drama! And who is this?"

That was the real point, of course. Who is this and why is he wasting his time with Emmie?

"This is Alex. Alex, I'd like you to meet — " and then she'd introduce Mr. and Mrs. Hastings, or Susannah, or Gretchen and Jonsy, or Leigh and David.

Alex could not have been more gracious. He shook hands, said the right things, told little anecdotes. An excellent guest.

Spotlights went on under the yellow tent. Venice danced with Michael, then with her father, and then with J Thiell. Emmie shivered. Michael's father frightened her, always had. "What relation is my sister's father-in-law to me?" said Emmie to Alex.

"Distant. Want to dance?" Alex did not hold her at arm's length, but face-to-face, as if they had known each other forever. The slow dance did not last nearly long enough. They split apart for two fast ones and Emmie, normally nervous when dancing, found herself free and easy. The rhythms entered every muscle. Still, the slow dances were better. She felt his muscles then, against her body, felt the threads of his suit jacket and the scratch of his cheek.

Alex stayed with her until the sun sank, leaving dramatic orange stabs through the violet sky. "Come on," he said suddenly, keeping her hand as if he owned it.

Don't daydream, she said to herself. Alex only latched on to you because he doesn't know anybody here except John.

She ran with him, at his pace, up the path mowed among the roses to the top of the Pearses' hill. A new and more distant horizon spread west. The awesome orange bulb of sun was back in sight, as if Alex could beckon to it, make it reverse. "The sun is a stage show," said Alex, "that never ends. It just rolls on down the road."

She wanted to kiss him. No, she wanted to throw him down on the grass and skip all conversation and —

Get a grip on yourself, Emma Elizabeth Pearse. You're going to make a fool of yourself. Now talk about that sunset. Talk about weather. "What are your plans for tomorrow?" she said, forgetting weather and thinking only of romance. "Michael and Venice will have left on their honeymoon, of course, but we'll be hosting all day Sunday. Want to come over for lunch and tennis?"

He gave her a strange smile, as sinking as the sunset. For a moment Emmie was afraid of him. The whisper of fear intensified her crush, as though fear were an integral part of love.

Daniel wanted to put his arms around Annabel, learn by touch what he could not learn from words. Her scent swamped him. He wanted to know the taste of her lips, explore her cloudy hair, find out if she'd be anywhere near him next September, if she wanted to spend the summer with him. Or life.

What was this love stuff, that had never touched you, not in twenty-two years, and suddenly you were drowning in it, with a girl you could not have?

Lie, he counseled himself. What does Annabel matter, anyway? You can never see her again.

But he did not lie. Because she mattered.

"Annabel," he said, so softly that she had to lean toward him, dangerously close, as if she were about to kiss him, not hear the most terrible words she would ever hear, "my mother and I are re-opening the investigation into my father's murder. We can prove that Hollings Jayquith had Senator Ransom assassinated."

She was blank. The words meant nothing. It was impossible.

"Your father," said Daniel, putting it simply, "had my father killed."

SEVEN

His mission, thought Annabel. His twenty-five wishes. I told him to make the wish. My pennies were so powerful, they brought me love. What if his quarter was that powerful, and brings him revenge?

He holds my father responsible for his father's death!

Her head reeled. It separated from her body, to float sickly above the laughing guests and the singing violins. Rosebushes filled the air with rich romantic perfume.

She tried to see deep into him, right up to the soul. "Daniel," she whispered, "you have to be wrong. You cannot have any proof. My father would never do such a thing."

Or would he?

How well did she really know Hollings Jayquith? How well did anybody? With his only child, he was loving, good, generous, wonderful. But in business? In the material world he possessed? What was he where she had never witnessed him?

A sliver of ice formed in her heart. For one thin sharp cold moment, she believed Daniel.

The shudder of horror — that she could betray her father by allowing the thought in her mind, that anybody could allow that thought — shook her.

"I'm sorry," said Daniel. He sounded as if he had been through not one wringer, but a thousand. "I didn't arrange this to hurt you. I didn't know who you were at the Egyptian Room. I should have, but I wasn't thinking along those lines."

He was sorry. Sorry that he planned to bring the world down on them. Not one camera shoved into her flinching face, but hundreds. And she would have to walk among the cameras and the gaping sightseers without batting an eye, because that was how, in America in the twentieth century, you showed courage. You faced the camera.

Annabel tried to get her thoughts in order. Find Aunt Theodora. Tell her. Go home. Telephone Daddy in Japan. Get lawyers. Prepare statements.

In the dark, Daniel's eyes were faint glints, his hair only a blur. I'm in love with him, she thought. He could say a thing like that and I'm still in love with him.

"Daniel Madison Ransom!" said Theodora Jayquith. "What a pleasure."

Oh, Aunt Theodora, thought Annabel. A tourist like all the rest, come to pay homage to Senator Ransom's little boy Daniel. Just you wait!

Daniel proceeded to shake hands with Theodora. "It's wonderful to meet you at last, Miss Jayquith." He sounded as if he meant it. "I'm looking forward to being on your show this week."

No! thought Annabel. He can't be going after Daddy that way! Not on Theodora's show! Daddy's own sister has to be a part of destroying him?

"My dear Daniel, you could have met me any time." The fabulous earrings dipped and swung beneath her hair. "We are going to have a fruitful discussion. You're my only guest. I'm giving you the entire show."

A gift Daniel would throw back in her face with violence. Is he enjoying this? wondered Annabel. Is he revelling in using her? I thought she virtually sponsored Senator Ransom. What history have they never told me?

"There's so much to talk about," said Theodora. "We'll show the film clips, of course, in memory of the tenth anniversary of your father's death."

"Murder," Daniel corrected her.

Theodora never responded to correction and she didn't respond to this one. "I'll have a thousand questions to ask, of course," she said.

"You won't need questions," Daniel told her. "I will have a statement."

Theodora's long gaudy laugh filled the air. The idea that a guest thought he could appear on her show and not deal with her questions was quite amusing.

Annabel was having difficulty catching her breath. Only a few hours ago, she and Emmie had kidded about possible Jayquith scandals. This was beyond scandal. This was murder. One of America's most famous. A trial for Senator Ransom's death would mean publicity beyond anything the Jayquiths had ever known. Her wonderful father. How would he bear up under this? She would have to be the brave daughter who stood by her father's side, right or wrong. And surely, her father was right, not Daniel.

She wanted to drive to her mother's grave. Race her car at a hundred miles an hour and take the turns on screaming tires and get there, and do nothing but sob. Fling herself down on the soft cemetery grass, kept as if grass mattered to the people who lay beneath.

Mama, I'm in love but it went wrong! He wants to ruin Daddy! Maybe he *can* ruin Daddy.

The ice shard in her heart grew larger and stabbed more deeply. Did she really want the truth? What if the truth . . . *what if Daniel was right*? Annabel scoured the thought out of her mind. She changed her Egyptian Wing wish. Forget true love. She needed truth.

Mama, how am I going to have it both ways? Love Daniel and still keep Daddy safe?

Mama . . . *is* Daddy safe?

From the shadows, Jade O'Keeffe watched them pair up, separate, and come together again, like froth on an ocean wave. Theodora. Annabel Jayquith. Daniel Madison Ransom. Emmie Pearse flowed up, the boy Alex in tow. Mrs. Pearse came and went. Annabel vanished.

These people had always had this. Their lives had fallen into place complete with beauty and wealth, excitement and grace. While she, Jade, had been left with dust and debris, dullness and dumbness.

And buses. She had thought the bus driver would never calm down when she said she was staying in Litchfield. "You don't have any responsibility for me," she said. "Stop worrying. I'll be fine." Jade did not want bus drivers caring about her, for heaven's sake. She wanted billionaires and television stars worried about her.

Jade had no difficulty crashing the wedding reception.

Fascinating, when you thought about it. There were clearly guards here. They looked like men who had also grown up in ugly industrial towns, hiding behind good suits not quite right for them. Jade was wearing her very best outfit, too, in fact, her only "best" outfit. She had bought it especially to meet Theodora. It was vivid, because Jade, like Theodora, wanted to stand out. She had agonized over the style, having no idea what was stylish in New York. She had been very overdressed for the bus ride up to Litchfield, but somewhat underdressed for a society wedding. Jade made up for it exactly as Theodora would: a swagger and a head thrown back ready to fight.

The guards had not seen Jade, but what hurt was, nobody had seen her. These people were so busy with each other! So involved, so flirty and silly. They were the champagne they drank: nothing but bubbles.

So this was the famous debutante. The billionaire's beautiful daughter. Annabel Hope Jayquith.

My cousin.

Annabel was so fair skinned that Jade was startled. Had the girl never in her life been in the sun? Did rich people not get tan?

Theodora held Daniel Ransom by the shoulders, lightly shaking him in a puppy owner way. Then she laughed. Horrible sound. Jade felt condemned, like an old building about to be razed.

Jade had planned to march right up to the woman; plant herself in Theodora's face, earring to earring. *So, Theodora. Recognize me?*

But a person who could laugh like that could do anything. What if Theodora saw no resemblance? What if Theodora found Jade's attempt to look like her insulting? Or worse, what if this had happened to her before? What if Theodora dismissed Jade, saying to her crowd, *these little fanzoids never give up.* And then laughed that terrible metallic laugh in front of her jet set, and turned away, forgetting Jade in a heartbeat.

But I, thought Jade, I can laugh like that, too. So I, too, can do anything. There are other ways to get in. Guards are stupid, and sometimes chauffeurs are stupid.

She found the chauffeur, the one who had driven Annabel and Annabel's skinny plain friend. "Such a headache," said Jade. "I simply can't last as long as I promised Annabel. Please just swing me by the house." With a stab of fear, she realized she did not know if the chauffeur had even come from Annabel's estate, let alone knew the way there or could get in. Too late to worry about that now. "I need to lie down for an hour," she explained. "Then come back for me, so I won't miss the rest of the party."

The chauffeur gave her a long look. For a moment Jade thought she had gauged this wrong. Overplayed her hand. Perhaps the Jayquiths were housing none of these wedding guests. Don't turn me down! Jade thought, hating him, too. I won't deal with bus drivers and limousine drivers! I won't, I won't! I want to deal with the real thing, with Hollings and Theodora and —

"Of course, miss," said the chauffeur.

Yes! thought Jade. She nearly shot her fist in the air and yelled in victory.

He's not going on Aunt Theodora's show until midweek. This is Saturday. We could blockade him. Aunt Theodora could just refuse to have him on.

"Annabel, how stunning! So interesting! Of course Venice is always interesting." Annabel was forced to gossip with an old Wythefield roomie of Venice's and chat with Mrs. Pearse. "I'm so glad Venice wanted to be in the country for the reception," said Mrs. Pearse. "So many wonderful memories here. So many including you, darling." She hugged Annabel.

Annabel had spent many holidays here, Emmie as many at Annabel's. Hollings encouraged his daughter to bring friends home, and he'd take them to dine in wonderful restaurants and shop in wonderful stores. They might find themselves whisked off to Switzerland or to the islands. If Annabel was in the mood for tennis, they would be popped into the limousine and driven out to the country.

Where will we be driven now, if Daniel has his way? thought Annabel. Out of the country entirely? What memories am I about to add to my store? The memory of the day our lives ended in mud and dirt?

No. Kicking Daniel off Theodora's show would add fuel to his argument. He could claim that Theodora — and her network and all the media — had conspired together to keep the murderer from being exposed. So Daniel had to go on. It was just that Theodora had to be ready. And it was up to Annabel to tell her. If Theodora would for one minute stop gushing over Daniel, Annabel would do so.

Beneath the soaring yellow tent, Venice and Michael were waltzing, which seemed the least likely dance for Venice. Venice thought that of all bridal traditions, the weirdest was to give the best possible party, invite your very best friends, have the best food, drink, and orchestra — and then *leave*! Honeymoon? Forget it! Venice would party until the last guest fell to the floor in exhaustion. By then the earlier fadeouts could be kicked awake and Venice could party for days.

Candice was dancing with J Thiell, and Mrs. Pearse with Gavin. And I, thought Annabel, I actually still want to dance with Daniel.

The hot flushing love had been replaced by such pain that she wondered if eighteen-year-old girls could have heart attacks. But it is a heart attack, thought Annabel. Just not one a medical doctor could chart.

People were changing clothes. Bridesmaids exhausted by their uncomfortable dresses, groomsmen sick of cummerbunds and high starched collars, were reappearing in tennis shorts and blue jeans. Annabel ducked inside, hoping for privacy in Emmie's room but of course it was packed with girls . . . every one of whom was listening eagerly to Candice's version of how Daniel Madison Ransom refused to have a Jayquith for a partner. "You poor baby," sympathized Candice. "I wonder what magazine the photographer was with. Did you recognize him, Annabel? He got you just as you started to cry, you know. What's going on, Annabel, honey?"

Smacking Candice had its appeal. But she'd better get used to this. In a few days, the whole world would be a Candice. "It's long-standing,"

said Annabel, implying that if Candice were anybody, she'd know already.

Annabel dropped her gown on Emmie's bed.
It slithered off to land on the floor, as heavy as
if a body were still in it. The corpse of my pre-
vious life, thought Annabel. She yanked on jeans
and a white blouse and jogged out of the house.
Theodora was dancing with J Thiell again. Annabel couldn't discuss anything in front of Mr.
Thiell. In a way she did not understand, Mr.
Thiell and her father were competitors, although
their businesses did not conflict. It was as if they
had a point system, and were always vying to
see who had scored highest.

Avoiding all eagerly signaling parents and
guests, Annabel swept across the lawns. She
would get Daniel to herself, somehow, some-
way.

Emmie and her new friend were teasing each
other over the racket selection in the tennis
locker. So was Daniel. He tipped a racket in her
direction, like a flippant private saluting his ser-
geant. Maybe he thought he could get out of this
because he was cute and he was Daniel Madison
Ransom. Of course, he *was* cute, and he *was*
Daniel Madison Ransom, and maybe he could,
because if she didn't get a grip on herself, she
would forget that her father came first.

Emmie and the cute boy took a court.

Annabel and Daniel were as close as they had been at the Temple of Dendur, but they were not surrounded this time by stones and strangers. They were alone in a garden in the soft summer dark.

Annabel tried to think of convincing arguments. The only argument that came to mind was that Daniel should wear white tennis shorts all the time. He had a great body, much stockier than it had seemed in wedding tails. Curls of hair on his legs and arms waited for her fingertips to brush them.

She swallowed. Who comes first — your father or a boy you don't even know?

Daniel broke a single white rose from the bush nearest him. In his large hands, it was miniature. One by one, he snapped off the thorns and then held the rose out to her.

She remembered the whorls and curls of his fingerprints, and folded her arms tightly to keep from taking the rose. Daniel, still holding the rose, put his hands lightly on her arms, but there was nothing light about the way they felt. He gripped her intensely, as if to draw out of her bones what he needed from her. The rose brushed her face, and he let go of it, and let his lips brush her face instead. They kissed. It was the lightest touch imaginable. It might not even have happened.

It wasn't enough.

They kissed again, and this wasn't a fraction enough, so they kissed each other's cheeks and foreheads and throats and hair.

The only name in her world was Daniel, and the only name in his was Annabel.

The dreams. The plans. They were happening. They were this stretch Cadillac, this serious bland-featured man in a *uniform*. He was not just somebody driving a car, he was a real chauffeur. He opened the limo door for her, she got in, and he closed it after her. *Yes!* thought Jade.

She sat very still, soaking up textures, willing herself to act as if she had always had this, and always would. The limousine seemed not to have gears. It oozed forward. Too quickly the drive was over. The chauffeur inserted a plastic card in a monitor and the immense iron gates swung outward. They would have crushed a car in their path. Lights tripped by the motion of the car came on as they passed, illuminating them like a ball field for a night game.

The house was not at all what Jade expected. Architecture in the Litchfield hills had been uniform: immense, elegant, white colonials with black shutters. There might have been a law that Connecticut houses must look like that.

The Jayquith mansion was a jagged startling

collection of separate buildings, connected by
glass halls, sharp-edged towers, and fierce stone
angles. Spotlights made pinkish pools, casting
overlapping shadows, like eclipses. Vertical sid-
ing forced the eye upward. It was a demanding
house. The house of people who got everything they wanted: even gravity obeyed them.
It was the house of people who said, I don't
care what anybody else does — I want windows in *this* place, in *this* shape, and I want them
now.

Yes! thought Jade.

She put her hand to the door handle before
she remembered that it would be opened for her.
She was impatient to leap out. It took the chauffeur forever to get out and come around and —

Somebody else opened the door.

They have a *doorman*? thought Jade. Like
apartment buildings?

But the man who had opened her door was
no employee.

He was — he had to be — Hollings Jayquith.

Jade's poise evaporated. She was a little girl
facing a big important man. She was trespasser,
he was king. Her stomach hurt and a headache
began, dull in the back, as if it were cutting off
her blood supply. The hours of practice failed
her. She could not remember how she had meant
to act. She could no longer imitate the fling of

Theodora's head, the arrogant stance, the know-it-all smirk that came before the killer smile.

"I expected Annabel," said the man, his voice the absolute reverse of Theodora's. Soft, but not nice soft. Mean soft.

"She's still at the reception," said Jade. Would the man recognize her? See his sister in Jade's bones and hair and glittering green eyes?

Hollings Jayquith said nothing more.

Jade forced herself out of the car. The man did not move to give her room. She was pinned between him and the vehicle. The chauffeur stayed on his side, resting against the open door. The men might have been her jailers, or keepers.

Don't let them see you're afraid, thought Jade. Prove you are one of them. She said baldly, "I am Jade O'Keeffe. I am your niece. I am Theodora's daughter."

The silence rested around them. It lasted, and lasted. It thickened like gelatin. He did not say, Yes, you are. He did not say, Yes, you look exactly like my sister.

"An interesting claim," he said at last. Hollings Jayquith did not glance at the chauffeur, but she could feel his wrath toward the man. The driver was not supposed to bring strangers onto this property. So why did he? thought Jade. But she must not drift off now. She must remember her purpose and pull it off.

She opened her handbag. It was too large; she
knew that from the reception; no woman had
had a big purse. She did not let herself look down
and scrabble among her stuff like an old woman
too confused to locate her change. Her fingers
located the envelope and she took it out and
handed it to him.

He did not take it.

She met his eyes, her rage threatening to take
her sanity. She opened the envelope. She had
never sealed it; she enjoyed looking at it too
much. She took out the two sheets of paper. The
birth certificate with Theodora Jayquith's name
under mother and no name under father. The
letter from a woman named Donovan who
had arranged the private adoption with the
O'Keeffes. The return address of Mrs. Donovan:
the Jayquith Hotel.

She held them up for him to see. Mr. Jayquith
did not react at all. He did not change his breathing, complexion, posture, or expression. He did,
however, take each piece of paper and examine
it.

"Those are the originals," she said. "But I
have photocopies in safe places."

That amused him. A very slight smile touched
his lips. "Miss O'Keeffe," he said finally, "come

in. You may tell me what financial difficulty
brings you here." He turned and entered his
house.

The interior was as black as a spider's parlor.
Anything could happen to her here, and no one
would ever know.

Or care.

Annabel and Daniel surfaced from their embrace. It was not easy. They had to decompress,
like deep-sea divers. Hands still exploring, eyes
still staring, hearts still stunned.

"My father," said Annabel, "would never do
such a thing, Daniel." She was genuinely calm.
She really felt like his friend. She actually was
comfortable with him. "It is out of character."

"How do you think a man amasses the kind
of fortune and power that Hollings Jayquith has?
By being a sweetheart? It's totally *in* character."

"How do you think a man is elected senator?"
she countered. "Not by being sweet, either.
Name one sweetheart senator, Daniel."

"My father."

"But what do you really know about your
father? You were twelve when he died. You have
to go on what people tell you."

Emmie, with wonderful timing, came between them.

It was all right with Annabel. She had to get

off the subject. She needed to keep Daniel's plans secret. Let nobody know until she herself knew how to stop it before it buried them like an avalanche.

"What are you two talking about?" Emmie cried. "You look so grim."

"Do we?" replied Annabel. "Then we'll lighten up. Who is the adorable boy you're with?"

"Oh! You must meet him! He was in school with John." Emmie dashed around the high wire fence that enclosed the tennis courts to bring Alex for their inspection. Daniel and Annabel waited in silence. After a moment she realized they were still holding hands. It was not her hand just lying forgotten in his, nor his hand which simply happened to be stationed on hers. Their fingers were tight, and warm, and hanging onto each other.

Emmie presented Alex and in spite of everything, Annabel was touched by Emmie's happiness. She pressed her cheek lightly against Alex's and told him what a pleasure to meet a friend of John's. The fact that she could not think of any Johns meant nothing; there were many people and names in Annabel's world and it was the worst possible behavior to admit you had forgotten some of them.

Daniel and Alex shook hands. "Where are you

in school, Alex?" asked Daniel, posing the standard question.

Interestingly, Alex did not comment on Daniel's status the way Candice had. Daniel might have been anybody. "I'm out!" he said. "We're all out! This is summer, in case you hadn't noticed." His words and ideas tumbled forward. "Let's play tennis in the dark," he suggested. "Emmie, turn off those stadium lights. We'll play by moonlight." Alex's enthusiasm was infectious; Emmie would already have done anything he asked; Annabel and Daniel needed somebody to let them stay together, to postpone the next scene.

Emmie and Alex played against Annabel and Daniel.

Daniel. But what about my father?

The moon was just right. Tennis balls flew like little spooks over the net. Annabel pretended the tennis ball was Candice, which helped her have a brilliant game. She hoped Daniel was impressed.

Then she thought: What difference does it make? We can't see each other. We can only plot against each other's plots, our families caught in a cycle of trying to destroy each other.

Love really is blind, thought Daniel Madison Ransom. I went and told the murderer's daughter. Now her father can cover himself. Prepare his own statement. Probably even appear on Theodora's show when I do. He'll make a relaxed indulgent rebuttal of a silly little boy's accusation.

Daniel averted his eyes from Annabel Jayquith. He had stayed here long enough to please Michael. He *had* to drive away. And he thought *Michael* had fallen in love with the wrong girl!

Daniel stretched dramatically. "Well, that's it for me, folks," he said cheerfully. "Great game. Nice to meet you, Alex. I've got quite a drive ahead." He waved the tennis racket. "I'm out of here."

He walked past Annabel Jayquith.

And was out of there.

EIGHT

I am the only person on earth who cares about me, thought Jade O'Keeffe.

She had known that, but never before been terrified by it. The chauffeur got back in his car and slammed the door as loud as a bomb going off. The car purred away, not like a car at all, but like an animal. Mr. Jayquith entered the black hole of the house. Every imaginable light was on outside, but not one single light was on inside. Jade pretended to be Theodora. Flung her hair and strode in after Mr. Jayquith.

The chauffeuer seemed to be the only employee. No maid or secretary materialized. Of course, it was evening. Perhaps they had been dismissed for the night.

His silhouette preceded her. And then she was in the light, too much light, a vast room with stone floors so highly polished she skidded. Ice-white walls were hung with dizzying modern art — great splats of color on immense canvases. She might have been touring a museum. There was no furniture.

They passed into a glassed-walled room, whose stone steps went down, across, and then up again. These stones were green; cold and isolating like the deep interior of a pine forest. An indoor waterfall cascaded from a monstrous mouth below hollow stone eyes from a Central American statue, silently watching human sacrifice.

The people Jade knew had yellow and brown plaid couches, fake leather recliners, and huge televisions. They had ashtrays for decoration and maybe a Disney World souvenir on the coffee table.

The living room was white. White leather couches, big as glaciers. White carpet on glittering white floors. Even the coffee table was immense white and leather. Nobody ever put a mug on that. Nobody here would even own mugs. The grand piano was white, not black like the one in the school music room. The single note of color was a brilliant scarlet, turquoise, and orange sort of blanket draped over a couch arm. It would probably not be called a blanket any more than the floors would be called "stone."

Two stories of glass faced the outdoors. It was

night, and lights staggered among distant trees
distorted black silhouettes and creepy un-
knowns. There were no drapes.

It had absolutely no feel of a *house*. Corporate
headquarters maybe. Art museum. But a home?

I didn't have a home anyway, she thought,
just a place to live. And this . . . this is not just
a place to live. This is a palace. He is a king. His
daughter is his princess. The house is scary because it's not really a house. But it's money.
Every wall and stick of it. *Money.*

Jade changed her mind. Forget blackmailing
Theodora. Who needed her? Revenge could
come later. Anyway, Theodora might shrug
over the papers in the lockbox. She had shrugged
when Jade was born.

But Hollings Jayquith . . . he had not
shrugged. He had brought her inside.

Jade shelved Theodora.

Mr. Jayquith gestured for her to sit, and when
she obeyed, he stayed on his feet. She was forced
to look up, a kindergarten child on her first day
of school, afraid and submissive. He looked
down, his thin features from this angle appearing
like so many knife blades.

At the wedding, she had thought J Thiell was
Mr. Jayquith. The father of the groom had
looked the way she thought a billionare should:

very broad, very strong, physically powerful.
Mr. Jayquith, however, had a civilized air, as if,
should he murder you, it would be done with
class. Mr. Thiell, like primitive man, would just
pick up a club.

Jade O'Keeffe had a club of her own.

It was another hour before Annabel could ex-
tricate herself from the wedding reception.
Good-byes were endlessly protracted. There was
kissing, hugging, touching of cheeks, and exchanging of summer addresses.

I won't phone Dad in Japan tonight, she
thought. I'll wait until morning. I'll call Theodora tomorrow, too. She's probably staying at
J Thiell's anyway. Ugh. I'm not calling her
there. Tonight I have to be alone.

The orchestra played on. Theodora was now
dancing with Michael, whose father moved in
Annabel's direction. Annabel knew what attracted Aunt Theodora to Mr. Thiell, but she
could not feel it herself. Mr. Thiell's power had
an underlying violence. She disliked being
around him. "Just a wonderful party," said Annabel, hugging Mrs. Pearse for about the doz-
enth time.

"You'll be here for tomorrow's activities, Annabel darling? We've hardly begun celebrating."

Annabel smiled lamely.

"You tell your father I'm furious that he couldn't arrange his life so as to be here," said Mrs. Pearse. "The man is a scoundrel."

Scoundrel? Yes, and far worse, if Daniel decreed it. Anything Daniel delivered to his fans would be believed. Especially on Theodora's show. People believed in Theodora. They trusted her to provide them with facts.

I kissed Daniel, thought Annabel. I loved kissing him. I want to spend my life kissing him. What am I going to do? What happens when the wedding photographer realizes that he has color portraits of Daniel and me together the week before Daniel accuses my father of murder? Will he sell some of Venice's pictures to the tabloids?

Mr. Thiell's hand settled on her waist. "So," he said in that dark shaded voice of his, as if they were both scorpions under the sand, "palling around with Daniel Madison Ransom, eh?" He smiled. Mr. Thiell never showed his teeth when he smiled.

"Congratulations," said Annabel, looking away. "Michael will make a fine husband. And you have a lovely daughter-in-law. Candice, dear, have you met Mr. Thiell?" She had the satisfaction of seeing Candice cringe as Mr. Thiell wrapped himself around her. Then she fled.

Tommy was waiting at the car. Annabel sank into the back with relief. Privacy and silence at last. A space in which to pull her thoughts together.

The car slid silently away from the Pearses' and down the quiet road to the Jayquith estate. She wondered where Daniel was. I'm out of here, he had said lightly. But they had not kissed lightly. They had not touched lightly. Which was fake? Which should she hold onto?

You can't hold onto any of it, dummy, she thought. Your father murdered his father.

She caught that terrible sentence in her head and killed it, biting down, smashing it. Daniel says that, she corrected herself. I was quoting Daniel. It's impossible. *Impossible.*

She was cold. Tommy had the air-conditioning on too high.

As cold as air-conditioning came the icy thought once more: *It's not impossible.*

Her suite had its own stairs to its own tower. An elopement room, she and Emmie called it. Nobody would see the ladder, Emmie liked to point out. The windows were not wired into the alarm system, because year-round, Annabel slept with them open. She would close them tonight, and weep.

For whom? For herself? Or for Daniel or for her father? How selfish am I? thought Annabel.

At least she was no longer at Wythefield. In the
dorm you could weep only in the shower, while
the beating of the water hid your sobs.

She had had love for a single night, and carried
it a week in her heart. What if she had been meant
for Daniel, and he had been born for her? And
their fathers together destroyed them?

The limousine did not feel bulletproof. She
felt no more protected than if she were wearing
the Egyptian gauze.

He's going to interview me, thought Jade.
He's going to decide whether to keep me.

Her hair prickled. This was it. She had no
other chance. She would never have another
chance. These people lived in a fortress. She
would never get in again, unless she said the right
things right now.

She tried to gauge this man who held her in
the palm of his hand. What must she do to win?
Should she be weak, so he could rescue her?
Should she be strong, so he would meet his
match? Should she flirt? Weep? Cling? Fight?

She must not mention money. If they thought
they could get out of this with dollars, they
would. The man assumed she was here because
of financial difficulties. She had to have other
difficulties — difficulties that would bind him to
her.

She must not make requests of any kind. Who knew what they would offer, if it were left up to them? Jade did not even have the vocabulary to name the blanket on the couch or the stone on the floor. What sort of vocabulary did these people have, unknown to her?

She had learned a lot from tapes of Theodora. Silence terrifies. People fill it. They say things they would hide if you yourself talked. She would make him use the words.

"My adoptive parents," said Jade slowly, aiming for a nice mix of pain and courage, "were killed in a car accident." She left it there. Let him go next. There was a long pause, while he waited for details. She gave none.

He looked down at the pieces of paper. He looked back at her. At last he said coldly, "I'm sorry. That must have been terrible for you."

It works! she thought. I can make him talk with my own short answers! "Yes." She blinked back tears she did not have, hiding a face shaking with desire and pretending a face shaking with grief.

She thought: What are the bedrooms like here? The bathrooms? I bet they live like Roman emperors. I bet Theodora has closets for miles! Or no closets at all. Whole rooms for clothes.

"Where did you get these papers?" he said in a quiet voice, too quiet.

He isn't sure, she thought. She looked up at him, letting her chin tremble as if she were about to break. She thought she saw something in his eyes she could only call hope; did Hollings Jayquith want her to turn out to be his sister's little girl?

Okay, why? she thought. Why would he want me? She took another risk. After all, each risk so far had paid off. "Have you always wondered?" she said. "Wondered what happened to me? If I was all right?"

He did not answer. He said again, "Where did you get these papers?"

"I always knew I was adopted. My parents always told me how proud I would be if I knew who gave birth to me." This was true. Jade left out the fact that she used to shout back, Well, *good*, because I'm certainly not proud of *you*! "When my parents died, these were in the lockbox with the life insurance document."

He remained standing. He looked away from her and across the wide empty room. There was something chilling about the unoccupied, unfurnished expanse of it. At length he studied her again.

Jade produced her trump card, her real proof. An old tattered Polaroid picture of Theodora, eighteen years ago, hairstyle caught in another time. Theodora, standing next to a fat middle-aged woman Jade did not know. In that woman's arms was a bundled infant.

Mr. Jayquith sucked in his breath sharply. For a long time he stared at the photograph. Whoever the fat woman was, he knew her. His eyes took that woman as proof, not Theodora.

"Please," she said brokenly, and let the word sit there, exposed and desperate. No description. No requests. Just *please*.

"I rather admire the way you arrived," said Mr. Jayquith.

"I would rather have been invited," she said, choking herself on the words, acting as lost and hopeless as she knew how.

After that, she quit using words altogether. She used tears and trembling, asked for tissues, and later a glass of water . . . much better than speech. And Theodora's techniques, memorized off the tapes, worked even with Hollings Jayquith. Into Jade's silence, he put words. And the words, syllable by syllable, accepted Jade O'Keeffe.

Yes! thought Jade O'Keeffe, and barely kept from shouting aloud.

Tommy opened the door. He seemed about to say something; he seemed in fact quite worried, but she could not concern herself with Tommy's problems right now. She stepped gratefully into the hall.

Every room at their country place was large. Her father hated being hemmed in. Ceilings soared, windows reached, floors stretched. To Annabel, each room had the serenity of great space, like cathedrals.

But this space was occupied. Something, somebody looming, reaching — she flinched as if it were another camera — but it was her father. "Hi, sweetie," he said.

Her father's presence actually made her jump with nerves. "You're supposed to be in Japan!" She had expected the night in which to think. But there was no time, after all. She would have to blurt out Daniel's plan. She would not have even one night in which to hold her romance in her heart, and pretend.

"Canceled," he said. He was deeply disturbed. She could see it in every muscle and sinew of his body. The angles of his bony face shifted with tension. No! thought Annabel. No, no, no, please God, don't let Daddy be guilty! Don't let him already be calling attorneys and planning defenses. Don't let Daniel be right, please, please, please. She could not bring herself to approach the subject directly. "But if you were in town, why didn't you come to the wedding?"

"I was dressing when something came up." He was almost deep-breathing, as he clenched his fists and then forced himself to fold his arms neatly. In the worst confrontations, the most appalling business nightmares, Annabel had never seen him so much as swallow hard.

"Sit down," said her father. "We'll sit in the French Room. I have something to tell you. Something that's been withheld from you for many years."

Annabel's life went black. It was not a faint, but a closing-in of total horror.

They never used the French Room. It was a formal parlor in which her mother's Impressionist collection hung. A room that almost smelled of lilies of the valley, although it had been many years since Eleanor Jayquith filled the vases. She did not want to hear whatever her father had to say in a room filled with the half-remembered perfection of her mother. "Tell me here," she said sharply. She knotted her hands together, and the bones of her fingers felt too close to the surface, as if they could snap if there were any more pressure.

He obeyed. They stood in the long white corridor that divided the traditional section of the mansion from the contemporary. "Listen to me, Annabel," he said, softly and passionately. "History never vanishes. You think it does. You think you have closed the book. But history returns."

History returns.

She put away her love for Daniel. She was going to have to stand by her father. She was going to have to survive this, and somehow love him anyway, and somehow —

"Theodora's history," said her father. "Eighteen years ago, when Theodora's career was just taking off, something happened."

Panic dissolved into disgust. If there was one person whose history she did not care about right now, it was Theodora's. "Daddy," she said in anger, "first I have something to tell you. We don't have time tonight for Theodora's history."

Her father frowned at her. He did not tolerate interruptions.

"Daddy, this is more important. Listen to *me*," said Annabel, raising her voice to force him into silence. "Tonight I met a boy who — "

Hollings Jayquith was astonished "A boy? Forget boys. We have a lot of ground to cover and a lot of decisions to make. Now. What happened was, Theodora got pregnant."

Annabel was well and truly silenced. Theodora as mother was even more astonishing than Hollings as murderer.

Her father went on. "Theodora was so upset

she couldn't even confide in Mother, and Mrs. Donavan and I were the only ones who knew."

Annabel's grandmother had been a thin harsh woman whose motto was "Be best or die trying." Annabel couldn't imagine anybody on earth confiding in Grandmother Jayquith.

"Theodora," said her father, "felt a career in television would be slowed down by a baby, and so Mrs. Donavan arranged an adoption."

Theodora had given birth to a child. Annabel practically fell over.

"Some couple from Ohio who had been trying for years to adopt, took the little girl," said her father. "Their name was O'Keeffe."

Annabel forgot Daniel. "Daddy!" she cried. "Why didn't you take her? Why didn't you and Mama bring her up? Why couldn't Aunt Theodora manage? Theodora can do anything! She could have had nannies and tutors! Who was the father? Why didn't she marry him?"

"That doesn't matter now," said Hollings.

Annabel had never heard anything so ridiculous. Of course it mattered.

"Because the girl is here. She appeared on the doorstep. She's quite a young woman. Very resourceful. Very pretty. Startling resemblance. Walks, stands, holds her head, just like Theodora." Her father's smile was confused, apprehensive. He said, "I couldn't send her to a hotel. I couldn't send her to Theodora, because Theodora of course is staying for the weekend with J Thiell. So — she'll be spending the night here. In the morning — well, I don't know what we'll do in the morning. I've left messages both at the reception and at J Thiell's for Theodora to call me right away, but she hasn't. I couldn't leave an explicit message, obviously, but she'll be here for lunch tomorrow anyway, that was arranged previously, and she can meet Jade then."

Annabel sank onto the rim of a pedestal that held a long, thin statuette. There was not quite room for both of them, but she needed to sit more than she needed to worry about sculpture. So many things had just been thrown at her. She could not sort them out fast enough. A sudden cousin! In the house!

"She's an impressive young lady," said her father. "I admit to feeling a certain amount of admiration. She has guts. She hasn't had an easy life and it wasn't easy reaching us, either. She seems like an acceptable girl, Annabel. Theodora will be excited to find that Jade has surfaced."

Annabel stared at her father. Was he *crazy*?

Theodora would be *horrified*! Did Daddy think
that Theodora had easily come to a decision to
give up a baby? Did he not know his sister at
all? The daughter Theodora had neatly excised
from her life *was back*? And he thought Theodora
would be glad?

To think that the girl had penetrated their
country place, their refuge from the city and
from all things painful. The house Theodora had
decorated, really, not Mama. A house of utter
and complete purity and cleanliness, where nothing homeless, or diseased, or damaged, or ugly
could ever intrude.

Theodora would be frantic.

How quickly this had taken place! How could
Daddy be sure this was the girl to whom Theodora had given birth? Daddy was the type to
insist on fingerprints and blood tests and genetic
analysis. What personality did Jade possess that
she could so quickly and so totally melt the ice
of Hollings Jayquith?

Annabel tried to clear her thoughts. She felt
like a helpless seabird landing in an oil slick. She
doubted, somehow, that she was going to find
an admirable gutsy long-lost relative. The story
sounded like straightforward gold digger to her.

Daddy can't know Jade's personality in one
evening! she thought. Then she remembered

falling in love with Daniel. Had she not been utterly, absolutely, sure of Daniel's personality in one evening?

"Daddy!" she said, remembering the rest of Daniel. "Daddy, wait." She dragged him to a stop. "Before we get into this, we have something else we really have to talk about. It's very urgent, Daddy. Tonight, I met the son of Sen — "

Her father took her arm to lead her to Jade. Annabel, dizzy with problems, felt as if they, too, were going down an aisle, to some new declaration, to make a new family.

"Annabel, don't bother me with your little crushes."

She stopped walking, but he did not. When had Hollings Jayquith ever changed his pace? Hollings was accustomed to overriding anybody's need, any time. *Don't bother me with your little crushes?* He continued to hold her arm, continued to stride forward, and Annabel was forced to skip up to him. *I'm bothering you with your survival, Daddy!*

"Family comes first," said her father briskly. "We seem to have a new member. At the very least, we have an unexpected overnight guest." He gave Annabel a strange smile that did not connect them. "I'm counting on you," he said, less sure of himself. "She's your age. You'll know what to do."

Me? thought Annabel. I know nothing. I didn't know that Theodora had had a child. What else in our history do I not know? That my father arranged the death of a man who threatened him?

NINE

Venice wore her bridal gown as if it were jeans. She strode around the rocky rim of the immense swimming pool, flinging her skirts out of her way.

"Your sister's a piece of work," murmured Alex. He flicked water on Emmie. Pool flirting. Emmie might have been plugged into a wall socket. Volts of electricity flung her heart toward Alex.

Alex in bathing trunks was male perfection. She yearned to know the details of his history. Alex was hard to pin down. His personality didn't settle. When Alex put his wet hands on her wet shoulders, she slid hers down the front of his chest. Oh, wow, thought Emmie.

"Emmie!" yelled her sister. "Get out of that water and come say good-bye to the Bruce-Newcombes."

Alex grinned and asked Emmie for a good-bye kiss, on the grounds that Venice might keep her a long time. No way, thought Emmie.

She was pleased when the Bruce-Newcombes recoiled from her soaking-wet hug. But she also had to say good-bye to Gavin's parents, and her great-aunt, and miscellaneous unknown guests. There were so many people here Emmie did not know. It was most odd to be hostess to a party full of strangers.

When she turned around, Alex and another boy were racing the length of the pool. Emmie watched his powerful form. What might his form be on their first date? She looked down at his neatly folded clothes, left on a bench because the cabana was full. Nobody, she had assured Alex, was going to rip off his bow tie. His wallet bulged in the pants pocket.

Alex kicked the end wall of the pool for his turn.

His driver's license would give his birthday. She could find out his horoscope. His address. Whether he lived nearby. To be in love you needed a few facts.

Alex, as he turned rhythmically to breathe and then dip back underwater, faced the other side of the pool.

Emmie slid his wallet out and flipped it open.

Jade was dying to prowl. To open drawers

and examine sculpture. Peek into closed places and fondle expensive things. But a mansion like this — it could have hidden cameras or motion alarms anywhere. So she touched nothing.

Actually there was little to touch. This place was stripped, as if the Jayquiths had been thoroughly robbed. If she had this kind of money — correction, *when* she had this kind of money — she would own a million things. Collections here, arrangements there, stuff on shelves.

Without doubt, Hollings Jayquith had known that eighteen years ago, his sister Theodora had had a baby girl. But the birth certificate had not convinced him that Jade was the girl. Nor had the adoption papers. The Polaroid: *That* had done it. The unknown fat woman in the picture meant more to Mr. Jayquith than Theodora and the bundled baby. After absorbing that piece of proof, he had sat beside her, and listened to her. By the end of the evening, he was saying that he would help her with Theodora! She could not believe it had been so easy.

The daughter would be another story. She was not looking forward to this late-night introduction to the daughter. Jade rarely made girl-friends. She knew she had to make an effort with Annabel, but the thought turned her stomach. This was the beauty Daniel Madison Ransom kept going up to. Ooooh! What a combination!

the guests had cried. Ooooh! what a beautiful couple!

Ooooh! You're making me sick, Jade had thought.

Her envy of Annabel had grown like a helium balloon, gaseous and soaring. She had expected Annabel's beauty to be exaggerated, due entirely to terrific clothes and an excellent makeup artist. She'd been wrong. Annabel was so lovely that even Jade could not take her eyes off the girl. But in Jade there was no admiration, only the building jealousy.

She got this. I didn't.

Jade was not quite in control of herself when, arm and arm, father and daughter entered the room.

Annabel had changed from her bridesmaid gown into simple jeans and a white blouse with interesting sleeves: rows and rows of holes. Probably an expensive handmade lace. Her arms were completely covered, and the effect was oddly sexy. I want a blouse like that, thought Jade. She wondered what it had cost. She wondered if these people would give her credit cards and charge accounts.

Jade stood slowly and carefully, as if a quick move would set off an attack. "Hello," she said. She was so afraid of the girl she had to clear her throat to go on. "I'm Jade."

The same unconvinced pause of the father was repeated in the daughter. "How do you do?" said the girl. Her eyes were soft and black like her hair. She didn't so much study Jade as waft over her. "My father tells me . . . that you think . . . you are . . . Theodora's daughter."

Jade wanted to slap her. Wipe that skeptical courtesy off the girl's face. "I know I am," she said, unable to hide her hostility. She produced, again, her three proofs of identity. Again, it was the photograph that froze Annabel.

"Mrs. Donavan?" Annabel whispered to her father.

"She arranged it. She took the baby to the O'Keeffes. I don't know who took the picture, but that has to be just after the two of them left the hospital. See? There's the tip of Theodora's car in the background. She was fond of Corvettes back then."

Jade had not even noticed. How extraordinary, that they were finding more proof than she had. Who, she wondered, was Mrs. Donavan? Well, she didn't care. That was eighteen years ago. Then, in spite of the fact that Annabel had not welcomed her, Jade, letting her voice break, said, "Annabel, thank you for welcoming me."

Annabel took a long time forming her next sentence. She was tired, bored, or else a space cadet. Or perhaps had the personality as well as the hair of a cloud. Nothing there once you touched it. "Let me show you to a guest room, Jade," said Annabel. Still not welcoming her. "It's late. We'll have time to talk in the morning."

"Thank you," said Jade, lowering her head. She was outraged. Annabel had spent only a few syllables on Jade and then brushed her off. Stick this interloper in a guest room and don't waste time talking to her, that was Annabel's approach. She'll pay, thought Jade, forgetting her plan to win Annabel over.

"The Peach Room?' Annabel asked her father.

Mr. Jayquith nodded. "Good choice."

Jade nearly rolled her eyes. They named their rooms. Too much. "The Peach Room," she repeated. "How nice. But I'd love to see your room, too, Annabel, if you'd let me."

Annabel said nothing.

Mr. Jayquith, almost but not quite frowning at his daughter, said to Jade, "Of course."

Annabel appeared to be in a coma. Jade went out of her way to display more personality. Mr. Jayquith swallowed everything. Even though she knew it was the Theodora in her that fascinated him, she revelled in it. Hollings Jayquith, unable to take his eyes off Jade O'Keeffe! When Annabel led the way, Jade took Mr. Jayquith's arm.

Annabel's room turned out to be a whole house!

There was a sitting room, with its own views and fireplace, media center and music area. Jade was stunned by the size of the screen, by the control panel for opening beautiful silent cabinets behind which sat the components of computers, games, and speakers.

Its own stairway led to a romantic aerie with a bed so high it required a two-step stool. Like a fairy tale. A picture book illustration.

And the closets! This girl had made a lifetime occupation of fashion. Clothes forever! Clothes for any season and any occasion. Shoes to match everything. Fabulous, absolutely fabulous, clothes.

And what did she wear? Plain jeans and a white blouse. Got away with it, too. Instead of a teenager, Annabel looked like a sea princess, foam on a wave.

I want this room, thought Jade. I will have this room.

I want her father. I want his affection and his money.

I will have them.

The wallet was, indeed, full of facts.

The boy was not Alex Scott.

He was not twenty-two.

He had not gone to Harvard.

So who was he?

And why . . . *why was he here?*

Don't bother me with your little crushes.

Annabel felt homicidal. This Jade girl was standing in Annabel's own sanctuary, green eyes like an auctioneer appraising the value of every object. Long fingers with long crimson nails like a seamstress, hemming Daddy in, sewing him up, taking him for her own.

Daniel is no little crush, Daddy! she thought, shaking with anger. And what happens after Daniel goes on television won't be a little crush, either. It'll be an avalanche! Every one of us standing beneath it will be smothered.

"And what are those?" said Jade.

"Tall closets," said Annabel, "for evening gowns, long coats, and capes." I have Daniel to think about, and Daddy expects me to entertain?

To be invaded in her own room made her feel vulnerable. Surrounded. How could she dream or weep or whatever it was she needed to do on this terrible night when Jade's touch had contaminated the entire suite? Stop it, stop it, Annabel ordered herself. What's the matter with you? You can't take a hard day out on some defenseless stranger. Be nice. This may be your cousin.

Annabel was in the habit of talking to herself the way she thought her mother would have. She often pointed out good manners and better behavior and tried to listen to herself.

This may be your cousin, she thought again. Do I believe her or not? Anybody could order a birth certificate by mail from the city records where it was recorded. But first you'd have to know it exists. If I don't know, and if the tabloids don't know (and how they will love printing this, in every gory abandoned detail!), how could some high school girl in Ohio know? Unless she *is* the girl?

But it was the photograph that was convincing. Mrs. Donavan looked just the same. Mrs. Donavan ran the Jayquiths' houses. She was a huge woman, her bosom like a pair of watermelons, her waist vanished in time and pounds. She neither cooked nor cleaned, did no secretarial work and no driving. Mrs. Donavan made arrangements. She moved a chef here, sent extra gardeners there, saw that somebody was fetched from one airport and somebody else did not miss his flight at another.

She was also, it seemed, a woman who could be entrusted with the arranging of private adoptions.

Jade opened the high doors and gasped. Annabel had gone through a floor-length cape stage, and had them in hunter-green velvet, scarlet wool, concert black, and sock-it-to-'em hot mauve and purple stripe. Annabel knew the girl wanted to wear each one of them.

Stay calm, Annabel told herself. Put this maybe cousin first. Daddy is right, family is first, don't get bent out of shape.

"Theodora will be here for lunch tomorrow," murmured her father, eyes fixed on his new niece. Jade, still holding the corner of the scarlet wool cape, pivoted. Her features swelled as if she had been stung. A smile as harsh and cold as any Theodora had ever turned toward a television camera puffed up Jade's face. Annabel thought she looked like a viper about to flicker its tongue.

I've got to call Aunt Theodora myself, thought Annabel. I have to give her time to prepare. She's going to be in shock. God knows I would have liked time to prepare for Daniel's announcement.

Jade was now reading the labels on Annabel's Italian shirts. How horrifying it was, really. For the whole eighteen years of Annabel's life, while Theodora lavished attention and energy upon her niece, Theodora had had a child of her own . . . and chose to lavish nothing.

Annabel had never thought much about giving up babies for adoption. It was hard to imagine herself in that position. She thought of Theodora going through a pregnancy. Nine months. It was a long, long time. A school year. She thought of her own senior year at Wythefield — also nine months — and how it had absorbed her. At the end of nine long, intense months, Theodora had graduated from pregnancy just as Annabel had from Wythefield. Closed the door, walked away, never gone back.

But Jade had gone on, just as the Academy would go on.

Had Theodora ever wondered about her daughter? Theodora lived in the present as nobody Annabel had ever met. She lived in the news of the moment. Today's conflict, today's argument, today's leaders, today's stars. Yesterday was unimaginably boring, tomorrow couldn't be reported until it came.

It came, Theodora, thought Annabel. Tomorrow is here.

Jade moved on down the row of closets, and her father murmured low, just for Annabel, "I always felt guilty, you know. I never told your mother. Eleanor would never have understood the choice to give a baby up. Theodora didn't want anybody to give her a hard time. Your mother would never have let go of the subject. Theodora and I, though, we let it go. We never talked about it afterward. I never talked about it to Mrs. Donavan, either. But I always wondered. I think I knew this day would come. I think I hoped it would."

Annabel was touched. Her father had kept his sister's secret. But in his heart, he had continued to ponder the fate of a little niece.

Mrs. Donavan's voice came sharply over the intercom. "Annabel?" She sounded large even on the intercom, her big overweight voice lurching through the wires. "Telephone, Annabel. Private line."

Annabel thought how much the newspapers would have paid Mrs. Donavan to betray this secret. She wondered if Jade herself would betray it; if Jade understood how badly the fan-struck world would like a juicy little detail from Theodora Jayquith's youth.

Telephone. Private line. It was probably Emmie. *But it might be Daniel.* Annabel rested her fingertips on the tiny white instrument. She did not pick up. "Excuse me," she said courteously, hoping Jade would take a hint and leave.

"Jade," said Hollings, "I'll show you to the Peach Room. It's on the lower level, one hall from Annabel. When you wake up in the morning, you just run on over here and get Annabel up. Then we'll all have breakfast."

When do I tell him about his murder charge? thought Annabel. Over cantaloupe? As we butter the croissants?

Don't bother me with your little crushes, Annabel.

"Annabel?" repeated Mrs. Donavan. "Are you going to pick up or shall I tell the gentleman to call tomorrow?"

Down the hallway, Annabel heard her father and Jade enter the Peach Room. She shut her own door and actually rested her spine on it for a moment. The relief of being alone was tremendous. "I'm getting it now, Mrs. Donavan." She picked up the phone, "Hello?"

"Annabel, it's Daniel."

Her heart expanded to fill the entire suite, like a great bright silk balloon. Daniel! Oh, there had to be a way! She would talk him out of it! She would convince him of — well, who knew what, but she would.

"Annabel, is there any chance we could meet tomorrow?"

True love does triumph. He wants me. He needs me. He'll put away his accusation. I'll save Daddy. *I'll have Daniel after all.*

Theodora, Jade, and her father could deal with painful ancient history without her.

Daniel.

"Just tell me where," said Annabel Jayquith.

★ ★ ★

Mr. Jayquith did not actually give Jade an embrace, but he lifted his arms slightly, as if he had thought about it. "Good night," he said hesitantly. She knew he could not hesitate over much in his life, this man who controlled an empire. I, Jade O'Keeffe, I have shaken him up, she thought gleefully. And tomorrow, I will shake up Theodora Jayquith! "Good night," she said firmly.

The door closed between them.

Yes! thought Jade. *Yes! Yes! Yes!* She felt like a gold medallist in the Olympics, the national anthem playing behind her, the crowds going wild.

She did a cheer, complete with airborne splits and circling arms.

I will have this. I will have *all* this. I will *always* have all this.

Coming down from her cheer, she narrowly missed a tiny table that held an equally tiny, peach-colored phone. She could have lived here a week and not noticed it. Jade stopped spinning, and stood thoughtfully. Mrs. Donavan . . . phone call . . .

Jade needed all the ammunition she could get. She lifted the receiver and listened.

Emmie's heart was a crystal goblet, smashing on the tiles that wrapped the swimming pool.

All the undeserving world, her difficult sister Venice included, found love. But not Emmie.

Annabel and I joked, thought Emmie. We said, Sure, if he wants you for your money, who cares? Pay him.

He wants me for my money. And I care.

He lied to get in here! *And I care.*

He crashed the wedding. His I.D. is for some little northern New York community college. His name isn't Alex Scott. It's the other way around: Scott Alexander.

The boy in question vaulted out of the pool. Water ran down his beautiful body. He flung his hair back and bounded over like a wet, excited collie. "Come on in, Emmie. The water's great. I've lost three races now. Your friends are Olympic swimmers." He flung an arm around her, hugging her so hard her ribs ached. Her half-dry bathing suit pressed against his dripping trunks. He kissed her throat, and without warning, tipped them both backward into the pool. Emmie was molded against his body and then she was underwater. They nearly touched bottom with the force of their fall, and then lightly popped up to the surface.

They surfaced. Water sparkled like frost in his hair. How honest and open and handsome his grin was!

But he was only handsome. Not honest and open.

"So, Emmie," said the boy who was here on false pretenses. "Do we have a date tomorrow?"

Her heart pounded. Was he after money? Was he dangerous? Was he sane?

But if she confronted him and threw him out, she would be alone.

Was it better to be lonely?

Or to have "Alex" and pretend he was real?

TEN

Daniel wanted to meet at Tanglewood, where the Boston Symphony Orchestra played outdoors during the summer. A "shed" seated 6000, but 10,000 more could buy lawn tickets. Annabel had often gone to Tanglewood, but never to sit on the lawn. It looked like such fun, a picnic with ten thousand other people, laughing and lounging on the soft grass beneath the loveliest trees outside of poetry.

Nevertheless Annabel would have preferred privacy. You could not be private in a crowd if you were Daniel Madison Ransom. "How will we talk?" she said reasonably. "Ten thousand people will recognize you." What's he wearing? she thought. Where is he calling from? Wait until tomorrow? Impossible.

"Clearly, you don't wear sunglasses. I do. The full wrap variety. And a cap — British driving type. Plus hot-pink shorts and a white-and-orange-striped T-shirt."

"Ouch," said Annabel. "Will you look weird?"

"You bet. You'll know me, though, and nobody else will. Our cook will pack a picnic. I'll have folding chairs and a blanket. We'll be lawn listeners. We'll blend. People will think we're dull and ordinary."

"Where will I meet you?"

"Front gate. Two o'clock."

She said good-bye, and when his voice vanished, she actually kissed the receiver. She couldn't even laugh at herself. She and Daniel would have their own orchestra, and her heart would dance. They would lie on their backs on a soft blanket, staring through green leaves at a blue sky; they would talk about each other and sort everything out.

The ten-year-old murder would stay in the past, where it belonged. History. *History never vanishes. You think you have closed the book. But history returns.* Well, Daddy would be proved wrong. Annabel would close the book on Senator Ransom. She and Daniel would make their own history.

Guiltily, she tried to concern herself with Jade, Theodora, and the confrontation to come. But she was in love. Even a sudden cousin meant nothing. When she awoke in the morning, Annabel could not even remember what Jade looked like.

Again today there would be no grave-visit. There was hardly even room in Annabel's mind to whisper *Mama!* and she was back in daydreams of Daniel.

Four times she changed her entire outfit, from shoes to earrings. She had to look casual, but symphonic. Grass-stainable, but romantic. She must blend in, but stand out. Even with a wardrobe the size of Annabel's, these were heavy demands.

Annabel's heart flung itself toward Daniel. She saw the road curving north, her black Jag purring past stone walls and pastures of black-eyed Susans. Her plans swept past Tanglewood, flew through summer, took herself through college and Daniel through law school. Theirs would be a world-class romance. She even decided on the wedding. She would commission music. They'd have their very own march, their very own love song. Every rock star whose music she'd memorized would be there. She'd rent a stadium, and hers would be a dance to rock the nation.

Daniel Madison Ransom was worth it.

Annabel could not take the smile off her face. It was as if she had a whole new face, anyway. New curves, new hopes, new loves. "I'll be back around suppertime, I think, Daddy," she said. "It might be later, though. Don't worry about me." She closed her fingers around the car keys. She would leave now, no matter how early she arrived in Tanglewood. The thing was to be there, closer to the dream.

"You're not going," said her father.

Not going? The smile on her face folded up like a bed into a sofa. "Of course I'm going!"

"Annabel, don't be ridiculous. Theodora is arriving to meet Jade."

"But Daddy — "

"You're not going."

"Daddy, this is important."

"Annabel, family matters more. What can you be thinking of? Cancel it."

"Daddy! This *is* family! You're so wrapped up in Jade you have no idea what happened last night."

"*Nothing* is important compared to the moment that Theodora meets Jade. Some boy you met at Venice's wedding? Forget him. If you can't forget him, meet him next week. Theodora will be here late this morning and so will you."

"I think Aunt Theodora should meet Jade

alone. I don't think either of us should be there."

"You're just trying to get out of this. Your aunt needs our support."

"Theodora never needed anybody's support in her life," said Annabel. "This is *her* daughter, not ours! We've already met Jade!"

"When did you get so selfish?" snapped her father. "Jade needs you, too. You're putting a silly joyride ahead of her?"

"Jade needs me? Daddy, what is going on here? Have you even verified who she is? Do you know for sure this is Theodora's daughter? She has two pieces of paper that any reporter could scout out if he knew where to start! What puts her needs first? I have needs here, too. Which you haven't let me explain! What Jade actually is, is a trespasser you'd have arrested under any other circumstances!" Annabel didn't care about Jade. She didn't know why she was having this argument. She was burning to leave. Her beloved father was nothing but a gate blocking the way. Move, move, move! she thought.

"She is my niece," said Hollings. "Your cousin. Theodora's daughter. I showed Mrs. Donavan the photograph. She remembers the nurse's aide who walked them out of the hospital taking it."

Jade was real. It should have meant more to Annabel, and she knew it, but all it meant was more difficulty, now, when she wanted nothing but a clear road to Daniel.

"Jade should have been able to come here by invitation," said Hollings, "and not by lies."

"That wouldn't be your decision anyway!" cried Annabel. "It would be Theodora's. Let's not forget that Theodora gave her up for adoption eighteen years ago. Maybe Theodora wants Jade back there in Ohio."

"In that case, you will hear it for yourself. But I think Theodora must have wondered all this time, too. I think it may be a great relief to her to discover how her daughter has turned out."

"It won't be a relief," shouted Annabel. "It will be a nightmare!"

"I think Jade is sweet and needy, Annabel. I think Jade is — "

"Jade is probably a money-grubbing imposter! Daddy, you investigate your staff more thoroughly than this!"

Her father gave her a shake. It wasn't much of one. But it was the first time ever that her father had used force on Annabel.

I am eighteen, she thought again, as if her age, like Daniel's pennies, were a more powerful talisman. If I want to get in my car and drive to Massachusetts and meet somebody, then I will. "I have a date," she said. "Daniel and I are going on a picnic. When I get home, Theodora will have met Jade. If she wants Jade, I assume she'll take Jade home with her. If she doesn't want Jade, I assume you'll be giving Jade money and putting her on a plane for Ohio."

"I can't believe this," said her father. "What is the matter with you? You have sympathy for the homeless, for alcoholics, AIDS patients, and third-world refugees. You have sympathy for whales, for God's sake, and you don't have sympathy for your own blood cousin?"

"I have sympathy for the woman who gave her baby up for adoption. And bringing that baby back into the family is not your choice, and not mine. It's Theodora's. Meanwhile, I'm meeting Daniel."

Nobody upset Hollings Jayquith's schedule. "Who is this Daniel that you put him ahead of my instructions? Daniel who?"

He actually expected her to cringe and buckle under, as if she were one of his accountants. And here I'm on my way to save your skin! thought Annabel. "Daniel Madison Ransom," she told him. She loved saying it. The syllables were like melody. She couldn't help smiling. What was she arguing for? Wait until Daddy met him! He and Daniel were so much alike that —

"*What?* That screwball's kid? Annabel, I forbid you to get near that family. His father didn't have enough brains to come in out of the rain.

I never understood what drew the American public to that fool senator. His favorite word was *investigate*. As if Senator Ransom could tell truth from fiction. The guy was nothing but fiction himself. The only thing he was good at was parading his newest suit. Always starting some Congressional committee to 'investigate' something. What a joke. The man couldn't match his socks, never mind investigate an industry."

The world did not share that opinion.

Even Theodora did not share it.

Was Senator Ransom going to investigate you, Daddy? What would he have learned? What would I learn if I investigated?

Annabel was out of breath. There was too much happening. "Daniel," she began carefully, "is a very interesting person."

"I'll bet. Brought up by a totally insane mother! He'd be interesting all right. The Ransoms became famous because one of them got killed. Period. You will not see Daniel Madison Ransom. Not now, not later."

"Daddy! First of all — "

"Drop the subject, Annabel. Change your clothes. We're going to have lunch out on the terrace and I want you in a skirt."

Her knees were jelly and her heart was slam-dancing. How could he put this interloper Jade ahead of her? "I'm eighteen, Daddy. I choose my own friends." She held up her car keys. She had things to do, and if he thought for one minute that he —

But this was Hollings Jayquith. He *did* think he owned the world. He even thought that he owned his daughter, too. He picked up the house phone. "Tommy? Do not open the gates. Annabel may not take the Jaguar."

The gates that so neatly kept the world out of their country place would now keep her in!

Annabel got back to her suite without actually assaulting her father, only to find Jade right in her own sitting room. As if she lived here. As if somebody had given her permission to wander.

But perhaps somebody had.

Jade fingered Annabel's clothing. The Theodora-copied expressions were replaced by hot gloating. Jade slid hanger after hanger down the rod, caressing linings, reading labels. "May I borrow something to wear, Annabel?"

They might have been roommates at Wythefield.

"We're about the same size," added Jade. "I really don't have any clothing with me. I left my suitcase in New York. Even if I had the suitcase

I wouldn't have the right dress for this occasion."

Who would? thought Annabel. She could hardly bear to look at Jade. "Wear anything you like." Who really does come first? she asked herself. Daddy? Theodora? Jade? Do I? Does blood come before love? Do I really love Daniel? Maybe it's just a crush gone haywire. Maybe Daddy's right. Maybe the Ransoms have nothing to offer but —

No.

Her father had not met Daniel. Her father knew nothing.

Annabel looked out her eloping window. When Emmie spent the night, she loved dreaming up elopement schemes. She thought running away was romantic. She's right, thought Annabel. "That's a nice choice, Jade. Why don't you try that on in your room?"

"I don't mind dressing in here." Jade pirouetted in one of Annabel's favorite outfits: a wildly colorful short skirt and bejewelled blouse.

"It's perfect," said Annabel. "It's yours."

As a bribe to get Jade to leave, it failed. "Is it out of fashion?" guessed Jade. "I'll wear something else then."

Daniel would be at that gate in his pink shorts and orange-striped shirt, carrying a picnic and chairs . . . and Annabel was going to meet him. No matter what the obstacles. She wracked her brains for a way past the gates.

"How how do I look?" said Jade, with a taunting grin identical to Theodora's. Jade had put on hot-pink shorts and a tangerine blouse.

Daniel's colors. Jade had listened in on his phone call! For some reason that shocked Annabel as much as the idea of Theodora a mother or Hollings a murderer.

Jade laughed. Peeled off the shorts and blouse and threw them on the floor. "You wear them. You two would look so cute in matching outfits. Not that you'll get there." She put the jewel-studded outfit back on.

"Annabel?" Mrs. Donavan called on the intercom. "Your aunt and Mr. Thiell are here."

Mr. Thiell? Along with Jade she had to lunch with J Thiell? She could imagine that shadowy brain, like a dark computer, storing and categorizing every painful instant, saving it for some great cruel printout one day.

"Your father," said Mrs. Donavan, "wants you and your guest promptly in the sunroom."

My guest, thought Annabel. Give me a break!

Annabel gestured to the door, standing back so Jade was forced to go first, and go alone. The wide white halls stretched like prison entrances.

Jade felt naked. She wished she had a big heavy
coat to belt over her fears. She wished she'd been
nice to Annabel; an ally really would have been
better.

You screwed up, Jade told herself. Don't do
it again. This is the one that counts. Don't let
Theodora see you're scared. It would be like
letting a pack of Dobermans see.

The sunroom was a large stone porch with
glass walls. Acres of wicker chairs, flowery fabric, and ugly rooty-looking plants that turned
out to be orchids. There were a few beautiful,
heavily scented flowers, but mostly there were
repulsive brown plant fingers. Jade fought off
shudders. I will not be intimidated, she said to
herself.

Theodora Jayquith was actually there.

Jade had pulled it off.

The woman had come. She gave off energy
the way the sun gives off heat. What had that
fabulous suit cost? Were those huge green earrings that glittered like science-class prisms really
emeralds?

Twenty feet separated them. Jade stood as still
as a fawn in the forest.

The woman who had given birth to her was
trembling.

Yes! thought Jade, blinking hard over perfectly
dry eyes. The great unflappable Theodora.

Jayquith. Moved to tears over me. "I've hoped
. . . for so long . . . that somehow . . . we would
meet."

But Theodora Jayquith was not trembling
with tears. She was trembling with rage. She
was not even bothering to look at Jade. She was
glaring at her brother. "Hollings! How can you
do this to me! Who let this woman in these
gates?"

This woman? In spite of having wanted to be
a grown-up all her life, Jade hated that word
used on herself. *Women* could take care of themselves. She wanted to be a *girl*, who needed to
be taken in, and sheltered, and given money.

"Tommy — "

"Tommy? Our driver! He's fired."

"Theodora, listen to me," said Hollings. "The
girl has proof."

Theodora stood extremely still. To Jade she
looked as if she had died. There were no vital
signs. No breath, no pulse. "No," she whispered.

Hollings was angry. "Theodora, you knew
your daughter existed."

"No. I knew that the O'Keeffe's daughter existed. Do you not comprehend adoption, Hollings? *The O'Keeffes have a daughter.* I do not."

Jade's hate was so immense that she too
seemed to have no vital signs: She too neither

breathed nor bled. She just hated.

Slowly, uncertainly, like a beginner on a balance beam, Theodora turned toward Jade. She looked upon her daughter as if afraid of the glare, of becoming snow-blind. She closed her eyes against the sight of Jade and then slowly, hoping the vision would have vanished, opened them again.

Jade held up the birth certificate. The adoption papers. The photograph. She had been right in her instinct to play to Hollings Jayquith instead of to Theodora, and she continued on that path. "I'm so proud to be your daughter," she said huskily. Theodora cringed, as Jade had expected her to, but Hollings was touched. Sentimental fool, thought Jade. She could not help turning to see how the others were taking it. J Thiell, whom she remembered from the wedding, seemed richly amused. But Annabel —

Annabel was not there.

Jade hated them both. Annabel could not be bothered to waste her time with Jade's entrance into the family, and Theodora could not even be bothered to speak to Jade.

I'll fix you! thought Jade. The strength of her own hatred turned the world and her heart to ice.

ELEVEN

Annabel took her horse.

It was wonderful, like an episode in *Black Beauty*.

Annabel could not think of a time she had enjoyed herself more. Not once in her life had she even thought of disobeying her father. It was heady stuff. She would have to do it more often.

The wind lifted her hair off the back of her neck. Her thighs pressed against Snowstorm's wide flanks. They headed through the woods, fording the brook and following a narrow overgrown path off the estate.

Annabel and Emmie had separately gone through years of horsey stages. She and Emmie had probably ridden the same paths at the same time, but had not met each other until Wythefield. Emmie learned to ride at Hilltop Hunt Club and Annabel at Snowy Wind Stables, where she got her horses. Annabel had had

Snowy Night and Snow Star before she was good enough to control a big horse like Snowstorm.

Annabel emerged from the woods into a new-mown meadow. Surely the smell of horse and the scent of cut hay made the world's best perfume. She laughed out loud. "I'm coming, Daniel!" she yelled, as if he and his horse were just ahead, and out of sight.

A few miles later they came out onto Blackbrier Lane, where Emmie lived. Annabel slowed the pace, cooling Snowstorm down. No cars passed and in a few minutes she turned down the Pearse driveway. The place was jammed with cars and guests. For a moment, Annabel blanked out. What was going on? Then she remembered it was Sunday and second-day parties were beginning. There were people here for brunch, tennis, swimming, and even things like croquet and cards.

She waved to guests who were thrilled to see a horseback rider appear. It was perfect. People grabbed for cameras. Annabel and Snowstorm ambled past the tennis courts and she turned Snowstorm over to the stablehands. She went into the house by a side door, said hello to the housekeeper, and dashed up to Emmie's room.

Empty. No doubt Emmie was off with the adorable Alex.

When this is over, thought Annabel, Emmie and I will need an all-nighter to tell each other the details of our romances.

Throwing off the clothes her father had ordered her to wear, she pawed through Emmie's closets for something else. Then she rooted through Emmie's purse for keys and scribbled a note. *Taking your car. Explain later. Extremely extremely extremely very valid reason, lots of love, Annabel.*

Emmie had inherited Venice's last car, an open-topped Jeep so Venice could explore wildernesses. Emmie hated the Jeep, but Annabel drove with as much pleasure as she'd ridden Snowstorm. She hardly slowed for corners and she shifted hard, pushing the rpms way above the red line.

Dust settled on skin and hair. Well, a girl who rode horseback and took corners on two wheels to escape her father's medieval-princess-imprisonments had to expect a little grime.

How funny, she thought. Everything's going wrong, and yet I'm having a wonderful time! I should run away more often.

She reached Tanglewood ridiculously early. The huge parking areas were largely vacant and nobody was at the ticket gate.

An ordinary, old dark brown Buick with shaded windows pulled up next to her. What a dull suburban car. Why wouldn't you buy something snazzy if you were going to buy something at all?

She was totally unprepared to have Daniel step out.

He laughed at her expression. "Camouflage," he said. "They don't expect Senator Ransom's son in this."

She sat behind the clear vinyl door of the Jeep, soaking up the sight of him. He turned the door handle slowly, sensually. Annabel swung her slender ankles out, Emmie's fragile sandals clinging to her feet like a row of tiny seashells. Her thick hair fell forward.

"And I must say, I did not expect Annabel Jayquith in a Jeep whose hubcaps obviously spend a lot of time in mud."

She giggled. "I stole it."

He laughed with her. "Hey. I like a billionaire's daughter with a hobby."

Theodora would look at Jade with fascination, and then look away, sorting her silver and folding her linen napkin.

What memories did Theodora possess? In all her plotting and planning, Jade had not asked herself who the other parent was. But out there somewhere was a father. Was Theodora thinking of that man and that moment? What had he been like? What had Jade inherited from him? Why had they not married?

Jade did not have room for yet another worry. She was dealing with enough ignorance just getting through the meal. She didn't know which fork to use when, so she didn't eat. She'd give them no weapons to use against her. She was the one with the weapon. She existed. That was weapon enough.

It was a pleasure to manipulate one of television's greatest manipulators. "These are Annabel's clothes," said Jade. "I don't have anything nice. We were very poor, you know." She paused to look sad and lost. "Or didn't you?"

Theodora lifted her chin. "I assumed your parents would take proper care of you."

Jade waited a beat. "They didn't."

Theodora wet her lips. Jade liked that. In all the tapes she had of Theodora Jayquith, not once had Theodora flinched or stumbled.

J Thiell put strong fingers on Theodora's shoulder and closed them, as if she were a door he intended to shut hard. Jade would not have been comforted. Obviously Mr. Thiell and Theodora were an item, but Jade found him threatening, like a tornado not yet unleashed.

As for Theodora, Jade could not identify her major emotion. Theodora was controlling herself with visible effort, but successfully; Jade was unsure what the woman was thinking. "I wish you had written to me first," said Theodora.

Sure you do, thought Jade. Not because you wanted to hear from me. But to give you a chance to build more gates and fences. "I wrote several times. Nobody answered. I telephoned. Nobody put me through to you. I went to the studio. Nobody let me in."

Theodora did not respond to these statements. But Mr. Jayquith said, "I'm sorry." He sounded sorry, too.

Jade went to work on him for a while. "It's my fault Annabel is not here, Mr. Jayquith. I'm sorry I upset her." Jade knew perfectly well that what had upset Annabel was not being able to meet Daniel, and what *really* upset Annabel was the order to stay home, and what really *really* upset Annabel was having the gates locked. Jade, against whom all gates had always been locked, loved it that the princess in the story had faced a little pain at last.

"Where is Annabel anyway?" said Theodora, very glad to discuss her niece instead of her daughter.

"She's probably not able to handle having me

here," said Jade. "This is a great blow to her. She isn't used to sharing. She's probably afraid your love will be divided."

Theodora looked at the ceiling with great irritation. "Annabel is not like that," said Theodora sharply. "She's a dear girl."

"A dear girl in love with a turkey," said Mr. Jayquith. "Or at least, son of a turkey."

"She's in love?" cried Theodora. "With whom? She didn't tell me anything about it. She tells me everything, Hollings."

So, thought Jade. Aunt and niece can be buddies. But not mother and daughter.

Mr. Jayquith set his fork down so carefully Jade knew he would have preferred to stab somebody with it. "Would you believe the son of Senator Madison Ransom? Daniel front-page-news himself? She met him at that charity ball I had to skip that was held at the Met. Then he turned up an usher for — well, you must know him, J. He's your son's friend."

Mr. Thiell nodded, but absolutely no expression crossed his harsh face. Jade could not imagine why he was tolerated around here. The beautiful people should have higher standards. "It's only the mother who's nuts, Hollings," said Mr. Thiell. "Unfortunately they're a package deal."

"I will be interviewing Daniel this week," said

Theodora. "It should be fascinating. He has a prepared statement to read. I can hardly wait."

"A statement?" said Hollings Jayquith. He looked alarmed. "About what?"

"It is the tenth anniversary, Holl. And he and his mother are obsessed on the murder, of course. Well, who could blame them? Madison Ransom was a wonderful, wonderful man." Theodora shook her head, and for a moment Jade actually thought she would get tearful, as if the senator had just been buried. "His death did change the course of their lives. No woman ever wanted to be First Lady so much."

"Why didn't she run for office herself?" said Mr. Thiell.

Theodora laughed. "Catherine Ransom? Very old-fashioned girl. She stands by her man. Her man does it all, she's simply decorative. Now the man who will do it is her son. Her son is her life." She frowned. "I'm worried about Annabel, Holl. The Ransoms would be a very difficult family to get involved with."

"I told her. She didn't listen."

Theodora shrugged exclusively with her hands. "Girls in love don't."

"What statement could the kid make about the murder?" said J Thiell.

"My impression," said Theodora, whose impressions were quoted globally, "is that the boy and his mother think they have uncovered enough new facts to warrant reopening the hunt for the real murderer."

Mr. Jayquith swore. "That means me. It isn't enough I went through this ten years ago, along with every other businessman whose name appeared in Senator Ransom's notes. Now we'll have to go through it again. Senators will be slitting each other's throats to be placed on the new commission. There's always lots of publicity and reelection value in murder investigation. Prime TV time, too," he added, giving his sister what Jade could only call a dirty look.

"News is news," said Theodora.

The sunroom was heavy with moisture from the plants. It was a hateful place. Why roast in this thick air? Why not use the cold, shining white room? Jade resented the whole conversation. The Ransom family was just an easier topic than Jade. "May I go?" asked Jade as sweetly as she could manage.

They were blank.

"To the studio," she amplified. She made her voice worshipful and filled her eyes with adoration for Theodora. "Of course I never miss your television show, but this time I could see you behind the cameras."

Theodora looked unglued.

You don't want me there? thought Jade. Then

that's where I'll be. Count on it, Theodora. "Please?" she coaxed, sweetly, so that Mr. Jayquith would fall for her request even if Theodora didn't.

Theodora actually put a hand to her stomach, as if to keep herself from throwing up. She answered without quite looking at Jade, staring instead at the white orchids whose heavy scent was suffocating Jade. "Daniel is a celebrity. Getting him on the show is a *coup*. I will be very, very busy. The studio will be chaotic. I won't have the time to spend with you."

"I won't make you ashamed of me," said Jade, knotting her hands up where everybody could see.

"I didn't say I was ashamed of you," said Theodora quickly, proving that she was.

"Do you think," Jade turned to Mr. Jayquith, "that Annabel would permit me to borrow something of hers to wear into New York? I don't want to offend her any more than I already have."

"You may take anything you like," he said.

Mr. Jayquith was not arguing with her assertion that Jade needed something to wear to New York. She might really get to go with them! She would be in the real studio of a real network. She would take those elevators to the twelfth floor of the Jayquith Building.

She wondered if she should have her name changed. Jade Jayquith. Were the first and second names too similar? Or was it perfect? Would it be her ticket to the world?

The sun lowered like the flame of a broiler, toasting them. Daniel had a six-foot triangular tarp, which they kept shifting so Annabel's face would be out of the sun. He memorized the pale curves of her cheek and the pillowy way her hair fell.

The ancient history of his life seemed no more important than the symphony playing in the shed. He barely heard the music, certainly didn't care about it. He could hear Annabel breathe and see her eyelashes rise and fall. He knew how she held her hands to applaud. She wore no lipstick but even so he could see the print of her lips on the glass of lemonade he had bought her.

She told him about her father having the gates closed. About her horses and Emmie. She even told him about her grave-visits. She said she had never told anybody and he believed her. She trusted him. "We visit my father's grave a lot," said Daniel, trusting in return. "I hate going. That eternal flame — I hate it. It rules my life. I'd like to extinguish it." Usually he never let that thought finish its way through his mind.

He was supposed to honor his father's memory and he did . . . but oh, the price he paid. He wanted to live among the living, not the dead.

Annabel touched his cheek. Her fingers rested there, cool and soothing.

"It's always on me," said Daniel. "His fame. When I see the headstone, and read out his name, I remember all my mother expects me to do. I'm going to. I've promised her. But I really wanted — "

He could not believe it when he talked to her about becoming a doctor. He never told people his dreams. Especially when they could never come true. He was enrolled in law, not medical, school.

"Will you enjoy law at all?"

He tried to laugh. He was dreading it. There was so much reading in law school, and about what? Old cases, old arguments, old hatreds — his life was full of that now; what could there possibly be to enjoy?

She rubbed the small of his back.

A camera clicked.

Daniel went rigid.

"It's all right," she murmured. She smoothed his cap down over more of his face, and moved her face under it, too. Their lips were an inch apart. "They're not after you. We're just atmosphere. Smooching couple on grass at Tanglewood. We're going to go in some tourist's album."

"You sure? The media follow me something fierce. You should see it on campus. They even know my schedule. My dorm room. The hour school lets out for vacation. They love that one, because they get my mother hanging onto my arm." Had Annabel ever stared at his photograph, wondered what he was like, wished they could meet? He had studied her portrait, the famous eighteenth birthday party shot. His mother had actually taken the magazine cover and snipped it with scissors. "I won't have that murderer happy in his family," Catherine Ransom said. "We're getting him, Daniel. It's taking a decade, but it's here. We're bringing him down."

Daniel stared past Annabel into the sun until he was blind with light. The muscles in his jaw tightened. What do I do? he thought. Mother has a two-pronged plan. *A.* I open the investigation and flatten Hollings Jayquith. *B.* I make a name for myself beyond Darling-of-America and run for State Representative next fall.

Forget A and B. Play with Annabel and go to medical school.

"I never went through that," said Annabel. "Daddy believes in a low profile."

The things I could tell you about Daddy, thought Daniel. But he didn't. "We have to talk about it, Annabel." He blew out the air in his lungs to reinforce himself, and lay motionless, chest not rising.

"Breathe!" commanded Annabel finally. "I don't know CPR!"

"CPR's for heart attacks."

"What are you having, a lung attack?"

He managed a laugh. "A nerve attack." I'm in love with her, he thought. No! Wrong! I won't allow it.

I'm allowing it.

They spent an hour walking. They drifted away from the softly chattering or peacefully snoozing music-goers. A huge low-slung pine tree gave them wonderful bark seats. He was afraid to touch her, as if, should they kiss, they would set themselves on fire, or be set afire by others.

"This week . . ." Annabel began.

He pulled away from her. "I'm going into New York to do the show with Theodora."

"Will your mother come with you?"

What a thought. "No. She's staying at The Camp."

"I can handle Theodora," said Annabel. "I bet I could handle your mother."

Now there was a wonderful thought. A girl

who could handle his mother. He couldn't help grinning.

She kissed his laughing mouth.

He kissed her back. They pressed against the huge trunk, as if to draw on its roots for their own strength. "Daniel. Let's meet with my father first." She cupped his cheeks in her long, cool fingers. "We'll talk about what you and your mother have discovered. I'm sure it's just been misinterpreted. I'm sure we can" — she waved one hand around — "come to terms, or something. My father is a good man. Please don't hurt us, Daniel." Her hand floated back onto his cheek. "Theodora always has stand-ins arranged, so she has last-minute available guests. You can cancel. Please, Daniel."

This is the girl who rode a horse and stole a Jeep to get away from her father? thought Daniel Madison Ransom. No. No way. This is the girl who told a very nice story to throw me off balance. This is a girl coached by Daddy himself. I don't care what you do, honey, just get the Ransom kid off my back for a while. I need time to cover my tracks, destroy my evidence. That's what Daddy said to his little girl Annabel.

She isn't going to throw Daddy over for a man she's known an hour here and there. She's

Theodora's niece after all. That makes her an actress.

"At least don't do it on Theodora's show," she pleaded. "Theodora is his sister!"

"She's the best. She has the largest audience." Daniel said, incredibly tired. Annabel had sapped his energy even more than his mother, and that was saying something. "And anyway, if anybody was in collusion with your father, it was Theodora herself."

Annabel stepped back from him, mouth open with shock.

Daniel folded his arms and pressed them against his ribs to keep from surrendering to her charms. Charms, he thought. They are truly a medieval family, these Jayquiths, complete with imprisonments and potions and charms. "I'm going to make the statement my mother and I prepared. You'll have to deal with it the way we had to deal with my father's murder. There won't be any escape."

"I see," she said quietly. She rubbed her lips with the back of her hand. What's she doing? thought Daniel. Scouring off my kisses? So she's hurt. People get hurt in this world. I should know. I was the most hurt of all.

"But what about us?" said Annabel.

He did not know what she meant.

"Us," she repeated.

He knew what she meant.

They stumbled together, and held each other so tightly neither could breathe, but it didn't matter, oxygen was nothing.

Only love mattered.

TWELVE

"Gosh, Mr. Jayquith." Emmie's acting technique required her to give the phone a puzzled look. "Annabel hasn't been here. We're expecting her, of course. After all, we're giving parties all day. But I haven't heard from her." Emmie folded Annabel'a note in her hand and closed her fingers over it, a small child with a secret. She winked at Alex. There was a feverish excitement in Emmie today that made Alex even more edgy. "I'll let you know if I do, Mr. Jayquith," promised Emmie, who clearly wouldn't. She hung up. "Alex, you will never never never never *never* believe this."

Alex was finding the entire weekend something he would never believe. He had never expected to get so close to his prey so speedily. All because Emmie Pearse had a crush. Later on that would be messy, but later on wasn't here yet. He felt no guilt over Emmie. She was necessary.

She had opened the door for him and he wasn't about to let her close it. *I'm almost on top of him!* thought Alex. Hot rage filled his veins. He thought of his brother's lonely death, his brother's pointless burial. He thought of dying in your twenties instead of living out your life span. He thought of all the things his brother had planned to do.

He hardly saw Emmie, just enough to deal with her, just enough to plan how to steer her in the direction he needed to go. He hoped this nonsense would not last too long. He could not control himself for a long time.

They were outdoors, having finished a game of tennis at which Emmie slaughtered him. The word *prep* did not mean to Alex what it did to Emmie's crowd. He had spent his afterschool hours as a prep cook in a fish restaurant, breading shrimp and onions. No wonder Emmie's backhand was superior.

"What happened, Alex, is that they had an argument over Daniel. Mr. Jayquith actually tried to lock Annabel up! Can you believe that?" Emmie swung herself in circles around Alex. She had more in common with Venice than she knew. And the lies he had to tell! He had never done so much consecutive lying in his life. Hard to keep track of.

"Ooooooh, this is so exciting!" cried Emmie.

"Can you think of two families more interesting than the Jayquiths and the Ransoms? Can't you just imagine them married?"

"Married?" said Alex. "They haven't even had a date yet, have they?"

"No, but you have to look ahead."

Alex wondered how far Emmie was looking ahead with him. "Why would Mr. Jayquith object?" he said, feeling his way.

"I don't know," said Emmie, slowing down and frowning. "He usually gives Annabel everything and anything on earth." She pursed her lips into a pout. "Psychologically speaking," said Emmie, "although normally I despise people who analyze their friends, I bet Mr. Jayquith sees Daniel as the first real threat to his control."

"He controls Annabel?" Alex could not care less about Hollings or Annabel Jayquith but they, like Emmie, could get him closer. He thought of the weapon he had purchased, locked tight in his car. He wondered if he would actually do it. An eye for an eye, a death for a death, a murder for a murder. He would not know the answer until he actually stood face-to-face with his brother's killer, and found out whether he pulled the trigger.

"Mr. Jayquith controls the world," Emmie giggled. "Except us. Shall we have dinner inside? Mother is calling. Or shall we have it brought to us out here? Or shall we go to a restaurant — no, forget that. We have to be here when Annabel brings the Jeep back." Emmie danced again. "*If* she brings the Jeep back. Maybe they've eloped."

No facts Alex possessed added up with the assumptions Emmie was making. "Let's have sandwiches out here," he said slowly. He could not face more adults who wanted to know where he went to school and how John was.

Emmie was amused, and he did not know why, until dinner arrived. It was pretty far removed from sandwiches. Platters of beautifully arranged, garnished, whatever-they-weres. He would rather have gone to McDonald's. They settled themselves on the grass beneath one of the big trees, as old and twisted as sculpture. Emmie flirted. Alex thought of death.

"Annabel!" shrieked Emmie.

Alex jumped violently.

"Over here!" screamed Emmie.

Annabel, having parked the Jeep on the grass, blocking the cars of several other guests, ran gracefully in their direction. Alex was glad to see she had some sunburn. Always good to have a sign of normalcy.

"Your father," said Emmie, full of herself, "is just a teensy teensy teensy bit annoyed, Annabel."

"Who cares?" Annabel handed over the Jeep
keys. "It was worth it. He can be annoyed from
here to California. What a perfect day." She
looked at the sun, lowering in the early evening
sky, as if she and the sun had previously agreed
on the day's perfection. Annabel included Alex
in her terrific smile. "I'm in love," she explained.
He had the weird feeling of being one of the
girls, as if they were in the dorm at Wythefield
and he was about to get in on the really good
gossip.

Annabel flung herself down beside them. "I
have so much to tell you! We talked and talked
and talked and talked. About his mother, for
example." She turned her beautiful dark eyes on
Alex and he shivered slightly, the way no glance
from Emmie could make him shiver. "You must
have met Daniel's mother, Alex. What is she
really like?"

He panicked. How was he supposed to handle
this one?

But Annabel was too excited to wait for answers. She seemed a whole different personality
than at the reception, where he had found her
moody and retreating. "Then I talked about my
father — I still cannot believe this morning happened, Emmie; wait till I tell you about this
morning — and about my mother, and the
grave-visits. Then we talked about poor Michael

and his ghastly so-called family life and then we
talked about school and the seasons."

"Seasons?" said Emmie.

"You know, how in kindergarten you make
autumn leaves for fall and snowflakes for winter
and tulips for spring."

Emmie rolled her eyes. "Sexy topics."

The girls giggled in unison. "Speaking of sexy
topics," said Annabel, checking Alex out so
thoroughly he blushed, "are you two also in the
running for best afternoon in the entire world?"

Alex added another lie to a very long list. "We
might be." He attempted to look at Emmie the
way a potential sexy topic would.

For only a moment, Emmie dropped her pose.
There was a depth of sadness in her eyes out of
sync with the conversation. *She knows*, thought
Alex with a jolt. I said something wrong and
she knows. Why hasn't she done anything about
it?

"If I go home, do you suppose Daddy will
lock me in the garret?" said Annabel.

"You don't have a garret," said Emmie.

"He'll build one."

Alex had to laugh.

"Actually," said Emmie, seriously, "I don't
think he knows what to do next. You can call
the shots, Annabel. Your father is so upset about
your fight this morning that he literally doesn't

know up from down. He even said something about your cousin. You don't *have* a cousin."

"Oh!" Annabel hit her head with the base of her palm. "I forgot to tell you! I *do* have a cousin. She showed up last night! While we were blithely dancing under Venice's tent, this girl walked onto the estate claiming to be my cousin."

Alex could not believe he was being allowed to hear this.

"How can you have a cousin?" said Emmie. "You don't have any aunts or uncles except Theodora."

"Precisely. This is Theodora's illegitimate daughter."

Emmie's jaw dropped. "You lie!"

"Her name is Jade O'Keeffe."

"No way! Theodora had a careless moment? It doesn't sound like her, Annabel. There's something wrong with this picture."

"I totally agree. I'm completely in the dark. But I imagine once I get home, they'll fill me in. I was supposed to be there for lunch today when Aunt Theodora met Jade for the first time."

Alex picked up a section of the Sunday *Times* that had been left by the pool and flapped it open in front of his face. He needed a moment to deal with this.

"*You skipped the luncheon at which your aunt*

meets her own child for the first time? They won't fill you in. They'll bury you!" said Emmie. "Well, obviously, Alex and I are driving you home. Aren't we, Alex?"

He sat up. "Absolutely."

"Alex will be male protection in case your father goes berserk."

"Not to mention Mr. Thiell. Where Theodora is, there also is J Thiell. Something has just occurred to me, Emmie. Do you think *he* could be Jade's father?"

"Gag me with a spoon," said Emmie. "Could anybody actually touch that man? You know I think Michael's adopted. It's the only way that scary cold man could have such a marvelous kid."

Emmie was growing on Alex. She had a good eye. He got to his feet. "Give me the keys, Emmie. You two do the planning, I'll do the parking." He was so wired he could have started the car without the key.

"Ooooooh, this is going to be so much fun!" Emmie rolled over several times, like a puppy in fresh mown grass. "We get to see the fireworks! Check out Jade! Watch Theodora deal! Learn what kind of punishment one Jayquith gives another!"

Learn what kind of punishment I give, thought Alex.

★ ★ ★

Mr. Thiell claimed that business required him back in Manhattan and he left.

Mr. Jayquith said he had to make a few phone calls and he left.

Jade and Theodora were alone in the hot dripping sunroom among the reaching fingers of thick fleshy orchids. The queen of talk had nothing to say. Jade waited. Finally Theodora looked out the tallest window, her back to Jade. She took a long, deep, slow breath. Jade got ready for whatever was coming. "What is it you want?" asked Theodora Jayquith. The only distinguishable emotion in her voice was curiosity.

What is it I want? thought Jade. I want a life. I want money and splendor and fame and private helicopters, like everybody else in this family. I would not mind having Daniel Madison Ransom as well, and every single piece in Annabel's wardrobe.

Jade schooled all emotion out of her own voice. She replied with great care. She needed to produce an answer that would make the Jayquiths give her all the above. "A home," she said softly.

Theodora flinched. Then, "Are you out of high school?"

"No. I have senior year to go."

Theodora brightened. "You could go to

Wythefield. Annabel went there, of course. Loved it."

What was she supposed to do there? Pretend to like girls like Annabel? Watch them pretend to like her? "Boarding school doesn't appeal to me," said Jade.

The topic seemed to be closed. Theodora seemed unable to think of another one. Jade stuck with her strategy to make them do the talking. In a minute or two, she was just plain bored. She could not do the things these people came to the country for: She could not play tennis, she could not ride a horse, she could not swim. In any event, Jade hated the outdoors. It was full of bugs. She said, "It's been a difficult few days for me. I think I'll take a nap."

Theodora nodded.

"Please show me the way back to the Peach Room," said Jade, although she knew it perfectly well. She would force this woman to do things with her. They walked through the massive halls and living areas to the wing where Annabel's suite and the Peach Room were. "Is your room down here?" asked Jade.

Theodora shook her head. "Off the sunroom is a partially underground hall that becomes a wing you can't see from here. It's dug into a steep hill and has fabulous views. The roof is grass and meadow."

"They mow your bedroom ceiling?" said Jade.

Theodora actually smiled. "Not when I'm home." She pointed. "There's the hall." She stopped walking.

Jade knew the emotion now that Theodora was struggling to hide. It was fury. Theodora *had* forgotten Jade. Theodora could not believe that things had come apart, that Jade was a young woman who could stride right in and make herself at home. That Tommy the chauffeur had let her in, and Hollings her brother had allowed her to stay, and Annabel her niece had not made things easier by being there to soak up emotion. Theodora was outraged, she was boiling.

Jade did not let Theodora simply walk away. She kissed Theodora on the cheek and whispered, keeping her face and breath close to Theodora's face, "It's wonderful to have found you."

A tic began in Theodora's eyelid. Jade smiled and left her standing there, while by herself she walked to the Peach Room. She waited there a few moments and then walked right back, shoeless and soundless, to be sure Theodora was gone. The halls were empty, and the volume of Theodora's wrath had left no trace; the white cold space might just have been sterilized.

The huge mansion was so unpopulated.

Jade found it eerie. Why wasn't it bustling

with staff or guests? There was an incredible amount of room, but nobody around. Mrs. Donavan was only a voice. The chauffeur had stayed outdoors. The food in the sunroom had been arranged on the buffet before Jade arrived.

Jade ran barefoot up to Annabel's suite. Annabel wasn't going to rush home from Tanglewood, whatever that was. Jade loved clothes. Before she found the lockbox, her only goal in life had been to clerk in junior styles at the department store. Now she could own the fashions she knew from magazines and television. She could go to the restaurants and clubs that required such terrific clothes.

In Annabel's dressing room — it really was a room, complete with three-way floor-to-ceiling mirrors, balcony, and chaise lounge so Annabel could rest her tired feet between costume changes — Jade tried on outfit after outfit. She put on a long black gown, tight as a mermaid's tail, and worked her way through the necklaces to see which glittered the most.

Footsteps sounded on the stair.

Jade's heart leaped. Annabel? The steps were light as a girl's. But wouldn't she have heard Mr. Jayquith confronting Annabel? Could it be Mrs. Donavan? Theodora?

Jade scooped up the outfit still lying on the carpet, closed the lid of the necklace box, and stepped inside the tall cape closet, closing the door.

The doors were shuttered to air the clothes. The exceptions were two solid doors she was unable to open. Fur coats, no doubt. Jade peeked through the shutter slat.

It was the chauffeur.

He opened drawers, searching through them. He put several changes of Annabel's underwear into a brown paper grocery bag, a pair of jeans, a gray-hooded sweatshirt, and a couple of plain T-shirts.

Annabel's running away! thought Jade. She sent the chauffeur to get her dullest clothing. I've come on the very weekend that Mr. Jayquith is losing his daughter.

Why not replace her?

"Wait," said Annabel.

Alex waited at the end of Emmie's driveway, letting the engine idle.

"Hand me the car phone," she commanded.

"What are you doing?" said Emmie.

"I need Daddy's assurance that he's going to be a reasonable adult about this."

Dream on, thought Alex.

"Hi, Daddy," said Annabel. "I think we need to talk."

Alex could hear every word of the response.

Mr. Jayquith was not cool. He was shouting. "I think you need to be home, young woman!"

Poor strategy, Jayquith, thought Alex. If she were a business competitor, you'd offer deals. Billionaire or not, this is the time to offer your daughter a deal.

"Daddy, I have to tell you what Daniel has in mind."

"He has in mind what every man has in mind when he sees a beautiful girl," yelled Mr. Jayquith.

"He does not," said Annabel.

Alex bet he did.

"Where are you?" demanded Mr. Jayquith.

"I'm coming home," said Annabel, "but only if you agree you're not going to do anything like lock the gates on me again. Really, Daddy, you are not running a prisoner-of-war camp."

"My daughter stays home when she is told to stay home!" shouted Mr. Jayquith. "We had a family gathering of the utmost importance. Your priorities are completely confused."

"Forget that, Daddy. Listen to me! Daniel is going on Theodora's show tomorrow night and he's — "

"I do the talking," said her billionaire father. Alex could almost hear his teeth grind. "I could not care less what a Ransom has to say on Theodora's show or off it."

"Well, you should!" yelled Annabel right back.

From the backseat, Emmie stretched a long, thin freckled arm between Alex and Annabel. She switched off the Jeep's engine. Alex understood perfectly. The noise of the motor made it hard to hear Mr. Jayquith's end of the conversation. He and Emmie suddenly exchanged silent laughter, for the first time actually on the wavelength Emmie had thought they shared.

"Daniel is going to accuse you of murder," said Annabel fiercely. "On national television. The murder of his father, Senator Ransom. He says he and his mother have proof."

Alex hung onto the wheel, trying to figure out what to do about that.

"I repeat," said Hollings Jayquith, "I could not care less what those Ransoms say. In person, on television, or underwater. They put me through a wringer ten years ago, along with every other possible scapegoat for the senator's death, and I refuse to go through it again. I want you home, young woman!"

Annabel hung up the car phone. "I could murder him myself!" she said to Emmie.

But Emmie was no longer laughing. She was horrified. *Daniel Ransom thinks your father had his father murdered?*

Alex was so full of things to say that they

canceled each other out and he was mute.

"And you went out with him anyway? Annabel! The guy wants to destroy your father, and you too, obviously, and you go to Tanglewood and have 'the best afternoon of your life'? Are you nuts?"

She's in love, thought Alex. Anybody in love is nuts. I personally am never falling in love.

"Alex, get out of the Jeep," said Annabel. He obeyed silently. Emmie obeyed, too, but not silently. Annabel shifted over into the driver's seat and flicked the engine back on. "Emmie, I have to have the Jeep."

"Wreck it if you want. I hate the Jeep. I just think you're being very very very dumb and very very disloyal. How can you even think of going to Daniel right now? So what if your father's being a jerk? He's upset. Anybody accused of murder and suddenly acquiring a niece would be upset."

Annabel's reply was a shower of pebbles hurled by spinning tires.

"Annabel, how is this going to look?" Emmie shrieked. "Just what do you think you are going to do? Appear on Theodora's show with Daniel? Hold his hand while he accuses your father of murder?"

There's time, thought Alex. I don't have to

do anything rash. I'll get Daniel's private number from Emmie.

The bottom of the sun touched the horizon,
like a glass of blood spilling onto the end of a
perfect day.

THIRTEEN

She was dangerous. She had no judgment. She was driving like a maniac. Eighty-five on a country road.

Slow down! Calm down! Annabel told herself. Her hair covered her eyes and she drove on without removing it, fingers so tightly clenching the wheel she could not free them. Then the wind yanked her hair away, flinging it behind her head like a black scarf.

Just what do you think you are going to do? Emmie had cried. Appear on Theodora's show with Daniel? Hold his hand while he accuses your father of murder?

She was driving toward The Camp, so that must indeed be what she thought she was going to do. Annabel drove faster, as if the tires could throw her anger back against her father at the same time they took her toward Daniel.

The road in Connecticut was empty dull blacktop through close woods and occasional fields. In Massachusetts it would be lined with hundreds of antique shops, their spindly little chairs and cracked wooden chests out by the street for advertising. Cars would crawl by, debating which antique shop would have more goodies. Annabel's father did not shop. He commissioned. In the city, a European decorator had filled the rooms with silk, rococo details, and shimmering delicacy. Here in the country, a design so low-key, there was hardly anything there.

Would Mama and I have gone shopping? she thought. When we came to the country, would we have our favorite little haunts? Oh, Mama! what would you do about Daniel and Daddy? Whose side would you take?

There was a stop sign ahead of her but she had no desire to stop. She bounced on the hard seat. The engine roared in her ears and throbbed beneath her body. Annabel wanted to drive on and on, faster and faster, as if some distant horizon held her answers, if she could just get there quick enough.

A small boy was pushing a lawnmower across the approaching intersection. She could see the rust on the red body that covered the blades and the gray exhaust from the oil-deprived engine.

I can see it, she thought, because I'm on top of it.

The boy was about ten. He was fair-skinned and black-haired, like Annabel.

I'm going to hit him, she thought clearly.

She slammed on the brakes.

The tires grabbed and screamed. The Jeep left the road, missing the little boy, ripping through tall grass on the verge, bouncing right over a ditch, like a car in a stunt, and coming through beyond the stop sign. She looked back. The kid, still in the middle of the road, was staring at her. A woman was racing out of the nearest house, screaming and waving.

Nobody was hurt. She didn't want her license plate written down. She knew she'd been a terrible driver, she wouldn't do it again, they didn't need to call the police. Annabel rushed on, taking the first turn off the main road, slowing to thirty, taking another turn, and then stopping at last, knees turned to jelly and heart racing.

She had done no thinking when she took the wheel of that Jeep. No driving, either. She had just pressed the accelerator to the floor and let come what may.

There had been girls at Wythefield whose entire lives were conducted like that; girls shipped to boarding school because their parents had no idea what else to do. Girls who did drugs, got drunk, slept around, enjoyed vandalism, practiced shoplifting.

I'm one of them. I didn't even consider stopping. I didn't feel like it. I nearly killed a little boy.

When she could pry her fingers off the steering wheel, she opened her purse and took out a ponytail elastic covered in black and sprinkled with rhinestones. With the hair out of her eyes, she could see. Seeing helped her think.

What am I doing?

Just because I want Daniel, doesn't mean I can have him.

Just because I'm furious at Daddy doesn't mean I can desert him.

I want Daniel. He gave me The Camp's unlisted number. I could call him. Tell him what's happened.

What *has* happened?

I don't want his voice. I want his arms and his embrace and his lips.

Annabel was painfully thirsty. Her throat hurt. Had she screamed, just before she avoided the little boy? Damaged her throat?

I have to talk to somebody, she thought. But I have to show some kind of loyalty. I cannot, I cannot, I must not, take this to Daniel.

Annabel started the engine.

She would talk to her mother.

★ ★ ★

Their lives were harnessed by tight schedules.

Theodora had to be in New York shortly. She had Sunday briefings for the coming week; she must prepare for interviews other than Daniel's. She had a breakfast meeting Monday; immediately afterward, her fashion consultant would be bringing choices for the week's television shows; Monday lunch was with a publicity-shy best-selling writer she was coaxing onto the show.

Hollings Jayquith was headed for Miami. He had had his people change his appointments from Monday morning to afternoon, but that was the best he could do.

They were completely stymied by Annabel's refusal to come home. They were not in control and this did not happen to them. Jade thought they were like elementary school children who got in the cafeteria line only to find there was no lunch that day.

Annabel's eighteen, thought Jade. She's a grown woman. Forget her! She probably has two hundred credit cards, she isn't going to go hungry.

"I have to go," said Theodora. "Holl, telephone me the instant Annabel gets in touch. Jade, you'll stay here with Mrs. Donavan."

Mrs. Donavan, the woman who had sold Jade to the O'Keeffes, had turned out to be fat. Jade despised fat people. She could never look at them, let alone talk to them. Fat nauseated her.

She never wanted to talk to Mrs. Donavan anyway. Jade did not want to know more about the O'Keeffes. She did not want to know how they were chosen, nor how Mrs. Donavan knew them, nor what Mrs. Donavan had seen in them. Jade never wanted to hear about that life again. She wanted it to die, to be buried along with the dead O'Keeffes.

Besides, Theodora would not be back to the country during the week. Neither would Mr. Jayquith. They would forget about her if she stayed here with fat Mrs. Donavan. Jade had to keep up the velocity of her presence.

"Is there room in the helicopter for me?" said Jade.

Theodora stood still, looking somehow thinner and less bold. She did not answer. This time, at last, she was unable to hide her expressions. Despair and fury took turns on her face. Take this unexpected nightmare on the helicopter with her? Face everyone in the studio — and, momentarily, everyone in the media world — with her illegitimate offspring? Her secret?

She's afraid of me, thought Jade. If I touch her, I bet her skin will crawl. She'll get goose bumps from her own daughter's fingers.

Jade touched Theodora. With her nails. No flesh.

Theodora did not try to hide her shudder.

So much for putting revenge on the shelf, thought Jade. Revenge is too satisfying. This is wonderful. I could do this to her forever.

"Perfect solution," said Hollings Jayquith heartily. "Let me call Tommy to take you to the heliport."

"I'm not packed," said Theodora. "Neither is Jade."

"Jade doesn't have anything to pack. Jade, go to Annabel's room and take what you need. I'll have suitcases sent up."

Jade thought she would probably need a lot of jewelry.

The cemetery was old. In preparation for the Fourth of July, flags had been placed beside the stones of veterans. The brownstone Civil War monument, with its carved eagles and sad lists, already wore its black wreath. Honeysuckle covered the fence around the cemetery, its rich creamy perfume filling the hot summer air.

Annabel left the Jeep in the narrow gravel drive that wound through the cemetery and walked among the headstones to her mother's grave. It was by itself under an apple tree. The tree was out of bloom, and tiny green beginnings of apple decorated the old gnarled branches. "Mama," she said.

She found herself weeping uncontrollably. *Oh, Mama, you wouldn't believe how bad it is! I can't believe it, either.*

I've just found out so much. I've found out that Daddy doesn't want me to grow up and have my own life: He wants me to grow up and have his life. I find a perfect man and the only thing Daddy can say is he's pathetic.

I miss you. I want a mother. I want you back, but I couldn't be nice to Jade for five minutes even though all she wants is a mother, too. I didn't stay to see her meet her mother. I had better things to do. I had to see Daniel.

You'd love Daniel, Mama. He's so handsome and smart and funny. He's perfect.

Except of course for the minor detail that he thinks Daddy killed his father. Would you have married a man who could kill?

A dragonfly, green and sharp, flew past. Tiny brown birds sang from deep within the apple tree. Where briars leaned into the cemetery, a little brown rabbit crept onto the grass.

The peace she always found here came again.

You're right, Mama.

I have to go home, work things out with my father. Family is first. Daddy's right. I don't know what will happen with Daniel. But I have to assume that all things work out for the best.

They don't, of course.

It wasn't best when you died.

But I'll tell myself they do.

Annabel rested her hand on the top of the gravestone. The sun had heated the stone, and the warmth was comforting. *Good-bye, Mama.*

She walked slowly toward the gravel drive.

A man sat in the driver's seat of her Jeep.

Blocking the exit to the cemetery was a smoky-windowed deep blue Mercedes.

Another man stepped silently from behind the Civil War monument. A rubber Halloween mask covered his face. The curved nose and red-tipped warts of a witch stared at her.

She tried to run. Her heart ran; her mind ran. Her feet stayed still.

She tried to scream. Her tongue and lungs did not.

No one spoke.

The birds continued to trill. The sun continued to shine.

The Mercedes left the gate, crawling toward Annabel. Strong hands encircled her wrists. Strong hands reached out of the dark Mercedes' interior and she was tucked inside the car as neatly as a child in bed. Inside, the hands pulled a Halloween mask over Annabel's face, too. The sweaty slickness of rubber stuck to her face. The sick taste of it lay against her lips. There were no eye holes.

The car purred contentedly as it drove away.

Daniel sat on the steps of the immense log porch, staring down the length of the smooth lake.

The sun cast a glittering, setting reflection. It was incredibly beautiful.

I could be sitting here with Annabel, he thought. We could sit while the moon rises. See the stars, hear the wood thrush and the crickets.

He did not know what to make of these thoughts. Usually at night the only emotion he felt was exasperation because he couldn't see as well in the dark. He was filled with wanderlust, a great yearning need to move, to travel, to be gone, to forget.

He had gotten his pilot's license last year, and loved flying. They had a private landing field, but it was not lit for night. Where would he go, anyway?

Where did he want to go, except with Annabel?

He tried to laugh at himself. He had certainly laughed at Michael, when Michael fell so totally and irrevocably in love with Venice.

Daniel thought with a father like J Thiell —

a father too famous even to put a period after his initial; a father who owned two entire cities built for gambling — Michael could not have a soft, romantic side. He'd been wrong.

Months ago, when Michael and Venice were setting the wedding date, she had been wearing a brown leather dress, low cut and revealing. The waistband was eight inches of metal triangles, cinching her waist like medieval torture. Daniel had stared at her, thinking— my best friend wants to live with a woman who calls that clothing?

But Michael had never even seen the clothing.

Now Daniel knew how that felt. He summoned Annabel's face to mind — forget her clothes. He was swamped by the total of her: shape and beauty, eyes and laughter, scent and softness.

So this was love.

It certainly was bad timing.

What about the interview? How was he going to sound forceful and vengeful on Theodora's show when he was sappy and lovesick?

Where did they get that word — lovesick?

He was love-healthy. He wanted to work out and lift weights and row boats. The energy of love was amazing.

The phone rang.

He bumped up two steps, reached over to the table, and picked up the porch phone.

"Daniel?' said a voice he did not recognize.

Not the voice he wanted. "Yes?" He already wanted to hang up and go back to thinking about Annabel.

"You will *not* make your speech about uncovering the assassin of your father, Daniel. Your friend Annabel is in our hands. You go on television, Daniel, Annabel goes in the grave. She won't go easily, Daniel. It will hurt, Daniel. She'll be scared, Daniel. And in a lot of pain. You think about that, Daniel. Call the network. Cancel your appearance. Forget the whole thing. Or forget Annabel."

FOURTEEN

Jade was absolutely terrified.

Limousines, yes. Jets, yes. Helicopters, no.

The helicopter was bare bones. No comfy up-holstery. No backseat televisions or bars. She and Theodora were strapped into seats separated by several inches, and Theodora motioned for Jade to put earphones on: big heavy-duty black ones that covered the sides of her head. Classical music filled Jade's ears. Jade hated classical. Stupid violins. She looked around for dials to get a decent station, but there didn't seem to be any controls.

She had taken the headphones off, ready to argue, when the rotors began to turn. The engine felt as if it were actually inside Jade's seat. Her entire body was jarred. The noise of the blades increased until it was too much for her ears to contain. Drunkenly, the helicopter lurched, came off the ground a foot and hung there, as if

deciding whether to crash. Then it rose vertically. Jade had eaten nothing in hours, but her
stomach tried to throw up anyway. The noise
was horrifying.

She almost came out of the seat when something sharp poked her rib. Was the copter falling
apart? Was it a piece of metal or —

Theodora's finger motioned Jade to put the
earphones back on.

She obeyed. Inside the big, soft black pillows,
violins talked to her and the racket of the helicopter was more felt than heard.

If she did not look at anything, her stomach
sat quietly. The moment she looked out the window — there was far too much window in this
horrible little bubble — she knew they were
going to crash. Every part of Jade was afraid.
Her ankles were jelly, her stomach rolling, her
armpits sweaty.

Theodora opened a briefcase and read from
sheets of computer paper. She crossed her legs,
and reached without looking for a small bottle
of flavored Canadian water tucked into a neat
compartment by her elbow.

Jade had one, too. She took it out of its slot.
Icy cold. Clammy and even more threatening to
Jade's body.

The violins became a piano and then a row of
blatty horns. On and on the boring music went.

Never a drum, never a lyric, never a melody.

Rich people had white rooms and boring music.

Jade would be a rich person who knew what to do with money. She would live through this without humiliating herself, and afterward she would demand the limousine and Tommy.

Tommy.

What was it with the clothes?

If for Annabel's sake, Daniel had set aside any of his hatred for Hollings Jayquith, it was back now. Never had Daniel Ransom so loathed another human being.

He refused to give in to the desire to swear or scream. Through teeth pressed together so hard his jaw hurt, he said, to Hollings Jayquith, "You did this for a publicity stunt. Annabel told you what I was going to say on television and you came up with a sick, perverted way to stop me. Nothing will bring the country's sympathy to your side better than a kidnapped daughter."

He only thought he was speaking calmly. Actually the adrenalin was pumping so ferociously he was screaming. Never had Daniel gotten from Massachusetts to Connecticut with such speed. Driving, he had had the sensation that he was not using road surface; fury and fear lifted his tires right off the ground and he flew.

Daniel wanted to hit Hollings Jayquith a hundred times, like a punching bag. He wanted to deflate every bit of pomp and pride. Leave the man flattened, eviscerated roadkill.

"She hasn't been kidnapped!" shouted Daniel. "You just moved her somewhere. She told me about your trying to lock her up this morning. You are a sick family. What kind of father are you? Holding your own eighteen-year-old daughter in front of you? Using your own daughter for a hostage? You sick perverted disgusting — "

He was ready to launch like a SCUD missile. He actually had to hang onto the doorjamb to keep himself from going after Jayquith.

How much of this, thought Daniel, in a rational corner of his mind, is the culmination of my ten years' anger about my own father, and how much is about Annabel?

Hollings Jayquith had just as much energy. He paced the immense room in long strides, smacking one fist into the other as if he were the drummer for his own march, plunging his feet against the floor as if wading through snowdrifts. "Don't be ridiculous! I would never do that!" he thundered. "Who do you think you are, anyway? You think you're important? You are nothing!"

"I am the sword hanging over your head," said Daniel.

"Sword?" shouted Hollings Jayquith. "You aren't even a penknife! What have you done with my daughter? Why are you making up this insane story about a kidnapper? *Where is Annabel?*"

"I'm not making anything up! You're the one making things up. You're afraid of me. You're doing this to stop me. Well, you've succeeded. I'm stopped. I called the network and left word for Theodora that there will be no interview. But only temporarily. Only until you take Annabel out of this."

Mr. Jayquith threw up his hands. "Daniel, you have no evidence that I was involved in your father's death because *I was not.* You're a grief-sticken young man saddled with a grief-crazed mother."

It was the word *young* that got to Daniel. He was twenty-two. On his way to law school. He was not young. Dimly he imagined himself and Annabel together for life. She'd have Catherine Ransom for a mother-in-law and Daniel'd have Hollings Jayquith for a father-in-law. Not a pretty sight.

"I expect to be the target of nutcases," said Mr. Jayquith, dismissing Daniel. "Of course you may go on Theodora's show and say anything you like. Nobody except grocery store tabloid newspapers will react. *Now where is my daughter?"*

They were panting and perspiring like fighters in a ring.

"If you're correct," said Daniel, "and you didn't take Annabel, then she really was kidnapped."

"Why would kidnappers call *you?* I'm the one with the money."

"You're not the one with the story."

"If anybody kidnapped her, it's your insane mother! Catherine's probably gone off the deep end. Literally. We should be dragging that lake of yours!"

Daniel went white. For that was an expression his cousins used — your mother's gone off the deep end, Daniel.

The Camp was not a home. It had not been a home since Daniel was ten. It was a shrine. On the fat, yellowing log walls, polished daily like silverware, hung enlarged photographs: the senator with car company presidents and oil magnates, diplomats, rock stars, fashion moguls, and movie producers. On the immense stone hearth sat the sneakers from the last time Madison Ransom played raquetball. Leaning against the wall were his golf clubs, labeled with the date of his last game. Open on the cherry card table was a chess set, left at his last maneuver. The library book he had been reading was still waiting to be returned.

On what had once been a dining room table lay open photograph albums, like wallpaper sample books in a paint shop. The final album, the one over which his mother spent the most time, was entirely photographs of Senator Ransom dead. Every angle of the corpse and the bullet holes. A dozen shots of the senators who had gathered round in horror. A dozen shots of the senators who had fled. The ambulance arriving. The gurney being lifted. The funeral home. The hundreds of bouquets — from tiny handfuls of daisies to immense brackets of roses. Daniel on the left of the open casket. Daniel on the right of the open casket. Daniel kissing his dead father's forehead as they closed the casket.

Every time the cousins visited (actually they made a point of not visiting), they jerked their heads toward the album room and muttered something about Daniel's mother going off the deep end.

Could Annabel have driven to The Camp? Could his mother, displacing her hatred of Hollings Jayquith, have taken it out on Annabel? A long, narrow pier connected the back deck to the float in the lake. Nothing had ever been tied up to the float but quiet green canoes. Daniel had spent many a summer day sitting at the end of the pier, feet dangling over the water, a fishing rod in his hand.

It was, literally, a deep end.

He had taken his time getting home after he and Annabel said good-bye (a prolonged and physical good-bye if there ever was one). He'd driven aimlessly through the mountains, equal parts thrilled by his good fortune at finding Annabel, and by his bad fortune at finding Annabel.

Could Catherine Ransom have —

No. Catherine would have wanted him on Theodora's show no matter what.

"How could anybody know that Annabel matters to you?" added Mr. Jayquith. "You just met."

How *could* anybody know? thought Daniel. It was comforting in one way: It let his mother out. He had not said a word to her about Annabel. In fact, Daniel had not said a word to anybody about Annabel. Although Michael had guessed there was a girl, Daniel hadn't given him a name.

Only the people here, at this house, in this room, or at Emmie's, could know. That didn't narrow things. There had been three hundred guests at the wedding reception, and plenty of telephones for them to notify others.

★ ★ ★

They landed on top of the Jayquith Building.
That was how they avoided the sightseers in
the lobby. Jade took off the hateful headphones,
and got out of the helicopter exactly as Theodora did, putting her feet and hands in the same
places.

New York City spread around her. High as
they were, plenty of the city was higher. It was
unbelievably beautiful. It was eight-forty. Night
had almost, but not quite, fallen. Against a puffy
silver-gray sky rose the black silhouettes of sky-
scrapers, sprinkled with lights and dancing with
energy. The city went on and on, its jagged ge-
ometry pieces of heaven for a girl who had lived
in the middle of nowhere.

Jade lost interest in the country. Why would
these people waste their time under green trees
when they could be here? A new emotion possessed her and made her giddy. She could hardly
bear to leave the roof.

I want this roof, too, she thought. I want New
York. I want —

Her heart was full of yearning. Something hot
. . . pulsing . . . scary but rewarding . . .

I love the city, she thought.

Jade had never loved anyone. Never been able
to figure out what girls mooned about. One reason she preferred the company of boys was that

they certainly never wasted time talking about love.

I wasn't designed to love people, she thought. I was designed to love a place. New York, New York.

"This way," said Theodora.

They walked together toward a set of doors that were flung open by a man in a suit. Theodora never glanced at him. Another man in a suit took her briefcase and Theodora never glanced at him, either. Three women joined them now, also suited, but more gracefully. They might have been napkins stacked on a table for all the interest Theodora showed in them.

They, however, showed interest in Jade.

The haircut and the green contacts had been worth every penny. Their jaws dropped. Their eyes widened. They exchanged stunned looks with each other. They wet their lips and visibly held back smiles of fascination.

How will she introduce me? thought Jade. What will she say? Does she have enough nerve to tell the truth? Should I tell the truth if she doesn't?

How to play the cards. That was always it, in the end. You did not know what you were dealt until you were right there, in the elevator, getting off the elevator, facing the bright greedy eyes. And you had to play right or lose the only game in town.

The elevator moved without sensation and stopped without sensation.

The doors opened.

A woman stocky and wide in a black suit said, "You have an important phone call, Miss Jayquith. Your brother. Urgent."

Theodora frowned. "I was just there."

"Urgent. He said nothing else mattered."

Theodora was irritated. "I have things to do."

The wide gray and white corridor filled with people all of whom looked urgent. They all had things to do that *could not wait* and *must not be interrupted*. People with deadlines. People who mattered.

Everybody except Jade wore black. Black suits, black skirts, black dresses. All shirts were cream or white. Jade had chosen canary yellow from Annabel's closet. The splashy wild pattern looked like one of the paintings Mr. Jayquith had on his walls. She was a flower among funneral directors. They were New York, they were television — but she, Jade, glowed hot as the sun. Their eyes could not avoid her.

This is it, thought Jade. This is my moment.

This was how Olympic gymnasts and divers felt, poised at the edge of the mat, the rim of the pool. Their entire lives, their years of practice, came together for this instant, these few seconds.

And the world watched. It was worth anything, to have the world know you existed.

Jade recognized no faces around her, but she did not care who they were. They cared who *she* was. They recognized Theodora in Jade, and were guessing, exchanging gossipy glances, their curiosity sharp and quick.

They were fascinated, and not by Theodora.

By me, thought Jade.

She imagined rows of magazines in drugstores — *People, Famous*, all the rest of the celeb magazines — and on the cover, her picture. Larger than Theodora's, because the article — the lead article — would not be about the woman who gave birth to her. It would be about Jade herself.

About me.

Jade stood exactly like Theodora, the half-swagger, the chin up, the sassy control all there.

Theodora did not have to go to the phone.

The phone came to her.

"Yes, Holl," she said irritably, looking at her watch. "What's the problem?"

FIFTEEN

The ride was long. From the feel of the engine, it was also slow. They were not in a hurry. Slow driving attracted less attention. But it was a striking Mercedes. In Annabel's experience, people always looked at interesting cars; no matter how many you saw, you were interested in the next one. And no matter that the hidden estates were full of famous television actors, sports heroes, and assorted millionaires — they were still ordinary people, to whom a vehicle like this was exotic.

But the windows were smoked, and nobody would see that the occupants wore Halloween masks.

They had left her hands free. She wore no seat belt. She could hear only the hum of air-conditioning and the cozy thrum of the engine. She could not even hear the others breathing.

She was sitting against the door, and the man

was on her left against his door. With her right hand she explored the door. It was utterly smooth. Velvet, with no appendages. No handles. No ashtrays. No map compartments. She could have been in a padded room.

Neither man tried to touch her. Neither spoke to her.

She grabbed the bottom of her mask and ripped upward so fast she had it halfway off before one of them jerked it roughly back down. All she saw were the hands.

The ride went on.

Annabel tried once more to rip the mask off, but this time didn't even get a grip on the rubber before her wrists were forcibly lowered to her lap.

They said nothing.

Annabel said nothing. If she spoke, nobody would answer, and it felt safer not to let her voice out there all by itself. She would keep her voice inside, keep at least one part of herself safe and private.

What were they going to do to her?

It had to be about money. Her father certainly had enough. But would they release her once he paid?

Oddly, the mask was an aid to clear thinking. She could not see, nor even lift her eyelids. There was nothing to do inside her head but think.

At Wythefield campus, one other girl actually lived with guards. She had been the daughter of an Arab prince at war with all the rest of the Arab princes in his family. It was unusual to bother so much with a daughter. After four years of living with Soraya, Annabel found out the prince was not guarding his daughter from evil; he was preventing Soraya from running away. Soraya did not want to be wed to a sixty-two-year-old prince when she got home.

They had graduated, Soraya to great applause, for she was a fine scholar, and Soraya had been assisted by her guards into her limousine for a brief drive to the airport and a thirty-hour flight to her wedding in a far country.

I promised Soraya I'd write, thought Annabel. I never did.

There would be a long list of things she would never do.

The car slowed for a speed bump. She had a sense of frequent turning, and altogether counted six more speed bumps. Where on earth did you find speed bumps? Hospital entrances? Boarding school campuses? Elementary school bus lots? Did airports have speed bumps? Were they going to fly somewhere?

Annabel was accustomed to private planes and helicopters, private yachts and elevators. She knew many people who came and went with anonymity using their own entrances and exits to the world.

An exit from the world.

It would be a small plane. They would wear their Halloween masks. They would take hers off at the last minute, so she could see what was happening. They would open the plane door, give her a gentle push. She would cling screaming to the opening of the door, trying to stay with them. We thought you wanted to leave, Annabel. And she would fall a mile, or two miles, watching the earth grow closer. Plenty of time to wonder how it would feel and listen to her screams vanish in the disinterested air.

But when the deep blue Mercedes stopped, and the men shifted, and her door was opened, she did not scream. She kicked.

She could have wished for better shoes to kick in. She had some wonderful high heels with pointed toes, and even one pair with a brass tips. But she was in sneakers. The man she kicked did not so much as grunt. He simply turned her, and with each holding an arm against her ribs, as efficiently as a wrestling hold, they marched her forward.

Wherever they were, there was nobody to wonder what she was doing in a Halloween mask.

Then she remembered it was nighttime. She

had lost track. It had been the longest day of her life since the day of her mother's funeral.

She was walked over grass. She crossed a brief stretch of pavement, she took, perhaps two steps on cement, and was back on grass. It was not mowed but tickled up to her knees. Pavement again, a single pace, and now the men half-lifted her, and they went up eight wide, deep stair treads. Stairs that were slick, like marble.

They stopped, and one man released his side, turning his grip over to the other. She heard the unmistakable metallic thud of heavy chain links collapsing against each other. A lock turned and a door opened.

Wonderful. Once she was on the inside, they would chain it again.

They tucked her fingers around paper. "Hold this." A whisper, revealing nothing of the speaker. Not the slick decorative paper bag of department stores, but the heavy paper of grocery bags.

They set Annabel inside the door, closed it, locked it, and chained it.

She dropped the bag and ripped off the mask.

She was in complete and utter darkness.

She could see nothing.

She knew nothing about her prison, except that one step behind her was a door. She moved backward to the door and felt the familiar push rod of door openers in schools and institutions. She felt all over the door. There were two doors. They fit well. There were no cracks. She pushed the rod down but nothing opened. Her eyes tried to adjust to the dark, but it was too dark in there for Annabel to see her hand before her face.

Annabel had never minded the dark.

Now she minded.

Who knew what was out there?

What pit — what trap — what fall of stairs — what hungry rat or spinning spider?

The silence was complete.

She heard no doors slam, no steps leave, no car drive away. Had those things happened, or was the place she was in too solid for her to hear?

She remembered the bag. Probably a bomb, she thought. They made me carry my own death inside.

She found the bag. Reached down. Jerked her hand back.

Inside was slithery and slippery.

Her hair prickled. Her skin crawled. She tucked her hands safely under her arms and even curled her toes up closer to her arches. She pressed her back against the door. At least she knew what it was.

After a while she slid down to the floor and sat.

She wanted them to come back. Those horrible silent men in their Halloween masks — she wanted them back. Any human was better than no human. How long would they be gone? Would they feed her? Take her to a bathroom? Bring her water?

How long would this last?

A night? A week? Until death?

Who had hired the men who put her here?

She had a taste of where Daniel had been for ten years: *Who hired them?*

She thought of Soraya. The icy doubts penetrated her mind again. Was she, too, under a father's control here?

Or did this have something to do with Daniel? With Jade?

The arrival of two such demanding people in her life had to be linked with her kidnapping. But what could either of them have to do with it?

She forced herself to touch the contents of the bag again.

Fabric, she thought. It's cloth. Small pieces of cloth. It's — *changes of clothing*. And — a bottle. Plastic one liter bottle. Unopened. How reasuring. It can't be poisoned.

She ripped off the flimsy cap and sniffed, and then sipped. Bottled water. Deeper in the bag she found jelly sandwiches.

Well, she was not meant to starve, die of thirst, nor wear dirty clothes.

That meant she was not intended to fall into a pit of knives among which rabid rats ran. So she ought to explore her prison. Find out what she was up against. Make sure that the other doors and windows were locked. Find a secret passage. Get out through the air-conditioning ducts.

Right.

She explored on her fanny, scooting forward an inch at a time. The floor was very solid yet it seemed to slant. Down toward what?

With the soles of her shoes she felt around to gauge what lay in front of her in the dark. She was afraid of getting disoriented, getting lost from the door and the bag. She tried to go in a straight line. Twice she backed up to reassure herself she knew where the door and the bag were.

The room smelled. It smelled old, mostly. Unused. It wasn't an unpleasant smell, as if something had died or rotted. It wasn't even a dirty smell. It smelled like an attic.

Her foot hit metal. She sat for at least a full minute before she could bring herself to put her bare fingers on the metal and feel it. A curved piece of metal, bolted to the floor. It was indescribably hideous to use bare hands to touch things she could not see. If only she had gloves! What if something trapped her fingers or bit them or scraped —

It was a seat. A seat whose velvety bottom flipped upward at the touch of a hand. An auditorium seat. Annabel stood up. Felt along the curved metal rim of the chair back. Found another next to it, and a row behind it.

They were keeping her in an auditorium.

Auditoriums had lights. She need only find the stage. That was easy, because now she knew why the floor slanted. Hanging onto the rows of seats, she worked her way forward.

By the tenth row she was less terrified of the unknown and could move her hands ahead, grip the next seat back, and walk her feet up to herself. That way, she thought, if there's a pit in the floor, I'll be hanging on and I won't fall in.

What's this pit obsession from? she wondered. Some long-forgotten television episode?

Her advancing shoe hit something. Not a hole. The sloping floor was no longer smooth. Somebody's hands, she thought, fingers, things reaching for me, grabbing my bare ankle —

She stopped moving. Waited for it to move first. Her hands slithered over the seatback and she swallowed a whimper.

But the whimper did not go down her throat.

Sobs overtook Annabel. If anything or anyone was out there, it knew that she had come apart. How weak her crying was. Like a small animal, wounded and waiting for the end. She stopped crying because it prevented her from hearing if the things in the dark were getting closer.

Swallowing, brushing her tears from her eyes, tightening every muscle to pull herself back together, she strained to hear.

Nothing happened.

There was no sound except her own convulsive breathing. She felt the edges of the obstruction with her foot. It was in pieces, whatever it was. She could shift it. If only she could see! She knelt, hanging onto the known safety of the seat-back and felt with her hands. Broken pieces of things, pieces that came apart in her hands, flakily turning to dust . . . pieces of ceiling? Pieces of plaster?

Was the auditorium falling apart?

Maybe I really do have to worry about falling into pits. Maybe the floor is caving in like the ceiling.

She worked her way over the pile of plaster. The auditorium was immense. Thirty-two rows. At last the rows ceased. She would be in that flat, open area before the stage. Wetting her lips, heart pounding so badly she wanted to yell at it, she walked across the absolute blackness, little baby steps until she found the stage. She clung to the edge of it as if to a rescuer.

She had figured out the first problem — where she was. Good guess, Annabel, she congratulated herself. She worked along the stage rim and sure enough, found exit doors. No exit light gleamed above them. Their push bars were also locked. Flattening her hands, she patted every inch of wall and finally located the light switches. Yes! She flipped them upward.

No lights went on.

She jerked the little tabs back and forth, back and forth, as if repetition could bring electricity into the switches.

I'm in an auditorium without electricity. What does that mean?

She found the stage steps and sat on the second.

She was filthy, hands covered with dust and grit. The place hadn't been vacuumed or swept in years. Where, in rural Connecticut, would there be an enormous, abandoned auditorium?

Annabel thought she would never find her way back to the paper bag and the drink of water. She had explored the backstage. She had found a small light panel behind the stage curtains. No lights went on from that, either. She bumped into all manner of frightening things in the wings, presumably props and pieces of wood. She did not bump into anything she could use as a weapon against her kidnappers or as a force against locks. She found half a dozen piles of ceiling fallen on the floor. She just hoped none came down while she was walking underneath.

Three doors opened off the stage wings. They were not locked, but they did not lead outside, either. She decided to go back and get the water and sandwiches and then find out what else was in the building. The auditorium probably did not have windows. But maybe the rooms behind it — music rooms? dressing rooms? bathrooms? — did.

When the kidnappers come back, they can't turn on the lights, either, Annabel reasoned. They'll have flashlights. So the thing is to get to know every dark inch of this place. Hide. Make them come after me, then run for the door.

It wouldn't work. One of them would stay at the door. Or they'd lock it behind them.

Still, it was something to do.

She returned on the opposite side of the auditorium.

For a building without electricity it was full of wires. She found them with her feet and with her hands. They were on the walls and the floors, winding under the chairs, looping across the aisles.

At the last row, when she met both wires and fallen plaster, it occurred to her to follow the wires with her hands. The wires traveled up a big support beam and buried themselves in something that felt like Play-Doh.

She was back at the paper bag, lifting the plastic bottle, unscrewing the cap, eager to feel water sliding down her dusty throat, when she understood.

Nobody was coming back. It didn't matter where she hid.

The building was not only abandoned.

It was going to be blown up.

SIXTEEN

Hollings Jayquith jerked up the receiver. "Jayquith here." His breath came in shallow spurts. His eyes glazed as he silently gripped the phone. He touched the wall to keep himself upright. His skin went gray, a man about to have a heart attack.

Very slowly he set the phone down, as if it contained a bomb. He continued to stare at it. "It was the woman's voice you described, Daniel. She said the same thing. They have Annabel. They don't care about money. They want no investigation. They want silence."

Daniel pointed. "*You* want silence. The facts don't change, Mr. Jayquith. You still killed my father. And somebody out there knows it. Somebody who *has* to be on *your* team, Mr. Jayquith, or they wouldn't care."

Mrs. Donavan said, "Perhaps Jade's arrival has

something to do with this. The timing is convenient."

"I just spoke to Theodora in New York," said Mr. Jayquith. "Jade's with her. She couldn't be making phone calls. I can't believe . . . I don't know what to believe." He looked up, his eyes filled with pain.

But he was Hollings Jayquith and he pulled back immediately. "Except," he said harshly, glaring at the young man who had invaded his home, "I certainly don't believe Daniel."

The yellow dress really could have been a painting on the wall for all the attention it brought Jade.

Annabel Jayquith had been kidnapped.

Nobody else mattered.

Even the broadcast did not matter.

People were thrilled. Usually they dealt with news by wire. News by long distance. They talked about it, but they didn't make it. They saw films of news, but they weren't actually there.

Here at last, for these newspeople, was news in which they could participate.

"Absolutely not!" snapped Theodora. "Nobody here will say one word to anybody. We cannot have publicity. That's the point of this. The kidnapper is trying to stop publicity."

"How much money have they asked?" said a reporter, his eyes glowing.

"The tabloids had a photograph of Annabel crying because of Daniel Madison Ransom," said another. "Does he know about the kidnapping? Can we get a statement from him? That would be great, having their pictures together. Good story. Let's — "

Theodora would have crunched these people beneath her shoe if they had had the decency to get down where she could accomplish it. But where news was concerned, nobody had decency. That was not part of the news code.

"Theodora," said the incredibly thin man who seemed to be the producer of her show, "it is imperative that we announce the kidnapping. We'll interrupt the current programming. People out there may have seen something! You need fifty million people to know about this!"

"No!" She was not shouting but she wanted to. "We have to wait for the kidnappers to call back! They'll have more demands. No publicity! Do! Not! Put! This! On! The! Air!"

"Theodora, news is news. You cannot censor it. I've given — "

"Announce this," said Theodora evenly, "and you will be the murderer of my niece."

Television screens hung on every wall, silently and continually broadcasting. There was noth-

ing exciting happening in the world. Mild
weather, dull elections, stationary economy. But
if Annabel's kidnapping hit the air, the nation
would sit up and take notice. Another exciting
crime! And this one would have all the glamor,
beauty, and wealth a voyeur could ask for.

Ranks of phones littered every desk. It was
not enough to have several lines per phone. They
must spend their lives on the telephone the way
Jade had spent her life in school.

Behind Jade, men and women were murmur-
ing to each other. "I wonder how much money
they'll ask."

"Doesn't matter. Jayquith has it."

"Did you see that fabulous photograph of Annabel?" breathed a woman.

"Isn't she gorgeous? What a family! Tragedy
always stalks families like this."

Nobody looked at Jade. Twice people moved
her, as if she were a bookcase that needed shifting. She was in the way. Annabel, kidnapped,
mattered more. Theodora, once more, had totally forgotten Jade. Theodora, once again, had
put a niece far far ahead of a daughter.

Somebody brought trays of food and coffee.
There were sandwiches of every kind, dark,
white, or rye bread, big fat yummy rolls and
skinny diet slices.

People moved in and out, swiftly, importantly, every one of them busy and urgent, although what they could be doing, Jade could not imagine.

Nobody would kidnap me, thought Jade. Nobody would even bother to get me a sandwich.

Theodora was making a dozen phone calls. She was staying calm. She was showing great courage. She was made of stern stuff. Jade knew this because that's what everybody was whispering. But Theodora did not look stern to Jade. The perfect hair was in disarray. She'd yanked out the magnificent earrings and thrown them on the desk so they wouldn't get in the way of the telephone she'd glued to her ear. Instead of eating, she tore her sandwich into little pieces.

Once, Theodora did look at Jade. But did not see. Anything other than her fear for Annabel was blurred and meaningless. Her eyes had never blurred for the newborn she left in a hospital for somebody else to bring up.

Kidnapped? thought Jade. I wonder. Her own chauffeur got Annabel's clothes. There's no kidnap. Annabel sneaked off with Daniel. The only other possibility is that Mr. Jayquith was so mad at her he decided he'd *really* lock her up.

I could tell you that, Theodora Jayquith. I could rat on Mr. Jayquith and you could stop worrying and we could go home together.

But you didn't offer me a home. Not eighteen years ago and not now. You don't want to be my mother. You want to be Annabel's. You're getting ready to cry. I can see it in your eyes. And all your admirers here, they're getting ready to forgive the lapse of courage, because it's about a beautiful rich girl we're supposed to love right along with you.

Well, not all of us love Annabel, Theodora.

And not all of us love you, either.

I was willing to forgive you when we got off the helicopter. New York was so spectacular and I wanted it so much I was willing to shrug just the way you shrug. Now I hate you again. I'm in the room with you and you *still* don't know I'm alive.

You'll know I'm alive pretty soon. I can make phone calls, too. You'll suffer, Theodora.

Jade was enjoying herself.

When she heard of girls dying young, Annabel always romantically thought how awful it would be to die before you knew true love.

I have been loved, she thought. It was only for a few hours. And by a man who hates my family. But he loved me. And I loved him back.

I loved him at the Egyptian Wing. I loved him

that whole long, lovely week waiting for the
wedding. I loved him at Tanglewood.

She counted on her fingers. Nine days. That
was all. How many hours? She decided not to
count them. What did minutes mean, anyway?

She probably did not have many minutes left.
She wanted to spend them thinking of Daniel.

Nobody else mattered. That surprised her.
The aunt whom she revered and imitated —
Theodora was nothing. The father whom she
adored — Hollings was nothing. The nannies
and teachers, dorm supervisors and riding in-
structors — they were nothing. Her friends,
from half-forgotten girls with whom she'd
shared a class or a locker to Emmie — they were
nothing. Even her mother in the grave was truly
in the grave — and nothing.

Daniel was everything.

She let herself melt into the memories, as,
lying on the beach in the sand, she could melt
into the sun and the salt air.

Daniel.

I will be in the grave before long, thought
Annabel.

It would be no traditional grave. There would
be no satin-lined casket. No prayers. No flowers.

A building would be her grave. Its beams and

rafters, its heavy plaster, its two-story walls. They would cave neatly in on her. Crawling beneath a seat would not protect her from the velocity and weight of the walls and ceilings. Eventually a bulldozer would arrive. She would be just another broken piece.

Her beauty and her money, after all, could protect her from nothing.

Mama's beauty and money had not protected her from death, either, and Mama had been underground half Annabel's life. Annabel tried to wrench her mind from the horror of being underground, and think again of Daniel.

But now that she had started to think of her own death, even Daniel receded from her mind.

Death did not terrify Annabel as much as dying alone. Alone and in utter darkness, with no clue. No warning. Somebody somewhere would flick the switch. Electricity would course through those wires. Plastic explosives would be set off. In milliseconds the building would come down.

Nobody would hold her hand. Nobody would share her fear.

Would it hurt? Or would it happen so quickly she would not have time to feel or think or grieve?

Another demand took over. Sleep. Her ex-

hausted body wanted to be unconscious. Perhaps
that was better. Perhaps she should be asleep
when the building went up, not even wake as it
came down around her.

But if she slept, she lost the only time left to
her on earth.

I have to go backstage again, she thought. Find
those doors, explore those rooms.

She was afraid to.

How ridiculous. Death was seconds or minutes or hours away and she was still afraid to
put one foot ahead of another. What could be
out there worse than death?

Sleep owned her. She could fight it no longer.
Her back against a row of auditorium seats, she
faded away, fingers wrapped around the water
bottle. She hugged it like a teddy bear. When
she woke, with a scream of her own, she could
not tell if she had slept ten seconds or an hour.
Her own scream terrified her. She lay panting
and shivering against the filthy floor. It was the
first sound the auditorium had heard in how
long? Years? What had made her scream out of
sleep?

Hands.

She remembered hands.

Hands that had jerked the mask down over
her face.

She knew those hands. Ten thousand times she had felt them helping her in and out of cars. Those were Tommy's hands.

Daddy had ordered this.

Right on Theodora's desk, open and accessible, was a Rolodex of telephone numbers. Jade flipped through and found the producers of the other networks' news shows.

Banks of telephones were everywhere. Voices blended into a cacophony of human speech, and nobody listened to anybody else, or even was aware of anybody else.

Jade called each of the other networks. If Theodora wanted the "kidnapping" suppressed, Jade would see that she failed. Everybody here could give in to Theodora's bullying, but Jade would not. She had power, and if Theodora expected to stay in charge of Jade's actions, Theodora was wrong. You want to call this a kidnapping? thought Jade. Fine, I'll call it a kidnapping, too.

She could guarantee the attention of the newspeople when she spoke the four names she had.

"Theodora Jayquith's niece," Jade said to three more networks, "Annabel Jayquith was kidnapped this afternoon. Daniel Madison Ransom is involved. Hollings Jayquith is about to make a statement from his Connecticut house."

She grinned to herself. Whatever anybody had
had in mind — Annabel, the chauffeur, Daniel,
Hollings, Theodora — it would be done now in
the public eye. It would be monitored and filmed
and preserved and analyzed. Their precious
white-walled, white-floored privacy was about
to be invaded.

I bet I'm not the only one who can break onto
those grounds, she thought. I bet every reporter
in America is going to give it a try now.

None of this was real.

Just a video in the dark.

Annabel stood up. She edged toward the stage
once more, still afraid of the floor she could not
see and the dark her eyes could not penetrate.
She carried the liter of water like a baby's bottle.

Tommy, who had driven Annabel all these
years, had put her in this building to die.

Who did *love* her, then? Did anybody? If her
own father could do this to her, who existed on
earth to love Annabel Hope Jayquith?

The worst thing was not, as it turned out, to
die without having found true love.

The worst was to die without love at all.

SEVENTEEN

A pile of debris had been pushed up against the door that led off the stage. Annabel had to stick her foot into the stuff to kick it away. Even though she knew by the smell and the way it crumbled that it was plaster, she hated touching it. What detonates the explosion? she thought. I could accidentally set it off myself.

Only that morning she and Snowstorm had ridden the trails to escape being closed up in her own house. What fun it had been in the sunlight looking up at the ink-blue sky and ducking beneath the thick green leaves of the sugar maples. In her imagination, they had done far more than canter down a leafy path. They'd leaped ravines and fled hordes of pursuers.

How romantic imagination was.

How filthy and dusty and frightening was the reality of prison.

In the end, she had to kneel in the blackness

and use her hands. She wrapped her hands in the pieces of clothing from the bag and it was much easier to touch unknown objects once her bare flesh was covered.

A long length of pipe had obstructed the door.

She shifted it, trying to figure out where to point it, and get it out of her way, all the while wondering if it was itself some sort of bomb, some sort of explosive. She didn't want her hands blown off. She whose hands could have been used in lotion or nail polish advertisements.

Stop worrying, Annabel told herself. It'll kill you as well as take your hands off so you won't know.

At last the pipe came free. She shoved the rest of the junk away from the door's swing space and came upon a small cylinder, smooth and instantly recognizable. A disposable lighter.

Annabel opened the door. Please let this be a way out. Please let me find a window I can pry open. Please let there be an outside door I can kick through!

How courteous she was being to the unknown god of prisons. Please don't blow me up.

She tried the lighter. A precious tiny yellow and blue flame danced between her palms. Annabel nearly wept. She had light. She could see.

Holding it low, she found three stairs going down. How easy to use them when she could see bottom. A black and dead space stretched beyond the steps, but what could be there to hurt her? With fire, with light, she had safety and knowledge.

Keeping the lighter as far from her face as her arm would reach, Annabel tried to illuminate the silent night of what was ahead.

It was full of people.

Theodora was giving orders. She had to get back to Litchfield and every route they offered her was too slow. She wanted to be beamed through time, like somebody on *Star Trek*.

Hah! thought Jade. Time and miles have you trapped, too, Theodora Jayquith!

It was arranged that the helicopter should get them to a small, private airport and a small plane should take them to northern Connecticut and a car with sirens should take them the rest of the way to the estate. Everybody at the television station loved this. This was action. This was the way life should be led. Nobody except Theodora was emotionally involved. Everybody else was just excited. They wanted Theodora on the scene, where it was happening.

The horde of TV employees and professionals were staring at Theodora as if the real Theodora were just a TV screen herself. Their eyes were glued to her. Nobody was looking at Jade.

Nobody had ever looked at her. This was no different from sitting in the tacky living room in Ohio, staring at the tapes. She was still a watcher. She was still unnecessary. Uninteresting. Unwanted.

On Theodora's desk lay a virtual phone store: a red phone, a yellow phone, a piano-key phone, a Snoopy phone, a view-the-insides phone. Jade wrapped a Kleenex around her hand and used the plainest phone on the desk. Black and utilitarian. She phoned the Jayquiths' country place.

Jade had barged into a family who already had a beautiful much-loved eighteen-year-old. They were not in need of another one. They might tolerate Jade, but they would keep her at a distance.

Don't let that Mrs. Donavan answer, thought Jade.

Mrs. Donavan didn't. Mr. Jayquith said, in a shaky, taut voice, "Yes? Hollings Jayquith here! Yes?"

Jade loved the panic in his voice. She was only sorry that she could not be telephoning Theodora to panic *her*.

Okay. What was a nice round figure? One million dollars? Five million? How should she have the cash delivered? Where? What should she do with it after she had it? There were more details to demanding a ransom than Jade had realized. She had telephoned first and was forced to do her planning while Hollings was waiting. She tried desperately to think up strategies for delivering money. Her own loud breathing filled the telephone lines.

She had not realized that mere breathing could be terrifying.

Hollings Jayquith begged. He begged for orders. He begged for instructions. He begged for information about Annabel.

Very interesting, thought Jade, He's taking this seriously. So he *didn't* have Tommy gather the clothes. He didn't lock her up. He doesn't know where she is. The only other person who could be giving Tommy orders is Annabel herself. Am I right? Does that mean Annabel and Daniel planned this? The wonderful Annabel Jayquith is putting her family through this on purpose? Annabel wants revenge, too? For what? Being told she couldn't drive the Jaguar?

Jade liked to think that a layer of scum covered Annabel's sweet beauty. That Annabel would make her own father and aunt pay a ransom. What a spoiled brat!

I should be so lucky, to be spoiled like that, thought Jade.

But perhaps she *could* be so lucky. If Annabel was really doing this herself (and what else could be the explanation?) once Theodora and Hollings figured it out, they'd never forgive Annabel. And then they would need another eighteen-year-old girl to take Annabel's place.

It seemed to Jade that no matter what happened, she would be a winner. She need only terrify these people with phone call after threatening phone call.

Around her bustled people so full of their own importance they heard nothing except themselves. "It will cost you, Jayquith," whispered Jade, her scratchy hoarse voice unidentifiable. "Be ready."

She hung up and dropped the Kleenex into a wastepaper basket. No beige plastic Rubbermaid trash can for Theodora Hollings. It was thick glass, an exuberant glowing tulip growing out of the floor, and it contained not one other piece of garbage. Some little minion must constantly empty it. Jade rather enjoyed seeing a crumpled Kleenex down there.

The office emptied of human beings, leaving Jade sitting alone in the large room with the silent television screens. These people moved like water, tides rising and falling, waves hitting first one office and then another.

"Theodora!" shouted one of the men in suits.

Theodora Jayquith neither turned nor slowed down. "Yes?" she snapped, striding away.

"What about the girl?"

Theodora had forgotten Jade's existence. "Oh," she said, blank and confused, trying to fit Jade into her calculations. "She'll have to come back with me. Get in, Jade." Jade might have been an annoying old pet dog, for whom allowances must always be made.

She climbed into the helicopter, her mind too occupied for fear. She latched the web of seat belts easily and paid no attention to liftoff. Inside the isolating earmuffs of music she connived. But she could think of no way to collect ransom money without being caught.

Okay. Forget that. Instead of actually trying to get the money, she would just stick it to them. Sneak out, find a phone, and terrify them. Rock their world a little.

Then she would come back into the room, all innocence, and comfort them. Jade would be the good girl.

Yes. That was better. Fewer loopholes, less danger. Better clothes, richer future.

Annabel's scream turned her lungs inside out. The scream alone should have brought the walls down. Instead it brought down one of the dead people lined up against the walls. The body fell straight, like a wooden frame, and brushed against Annabel before it hit the floor.

The little light in her hand flickered and went
out.

Annabel was trembling so badly she had no
knees left, no ankles, no muscles. She sank to
the floor and knelt quivering. The thing that lay
against her did not have enough weight for bones
and body. It was only cloth.

She was in the costume room.

They weren't people. They were ball gowns,
Pilgrim costumes, robes on hangers, leaning
suits of armor, and masks stacked on shelves.

She removed the costume from her lap as if
it had been a dead thing.

Again she lit the lighter. The costume room
had another exit and she followed that door into
a hall. This was relatively bare. Over the other
three doors in the hall were signs: BASEMENT
STORAGE, THEATRE OFFICE, MUSIC PRACTICE
ROOM.

It was like a quiz show: Behind which door
is the prize?

She went into the office, because her life had
been built around offices; her father had so many
of them, including the portable ones, the duplicates, so that he could work on plane or yacht
or car or country place or island home. Aunt
Theodora not only had her portable offices, she
had her mobile research teams and her myriad

phone lines. Theodora's and Hollings' worlds were lived by wire: Their lives, to say the least, were telephone intensive.

The office window was boarded up on the outside. The telephones still sat on the abandoned desk, but when she lifted the receiver there was only silence.

She must not use up her flame.

The little lighter could not go on for much longer.

She jerked open desk drawers as if she thought a flashlight with new batteries would be waiting for her.

Nothing remained but a few paper clips, a single blank envelope, and one pencil.

The fear had lessened. Annabel felt a sort of pride. She, Annabel Hope, who could have been only a poor copy of Theodora Jayquith or the heir of Hollings Jayquith, had faced this horror and taken action. Neither her father nor her aunt had ever faced real horror themselves. They knew about horror: Aunt Theodora had seen everything from war zones to famine camps, to volcanic explosions and inner-city riots. But she only talked about it. She only pointed to pictures of it. She herself had never experienced any.

For the first time in her life Annabel did not envy her famous aunt. If I get through this, thought Annabel, I will have done more than

Theodora. I will have toughed it out alone. No team, no backup, no employer, no plane, no bank of phones, no rank and file.

Just me.

And if I don't get through, I tried. I didn't lie down and give up. Well, actually I did, momentarily, but then I conquered my fear and went on.

She wanted to talk to Daniel again, tell him he had to be Daniel, not his mother's master plan for a dead senator. Live *your* life, Daniel, she thought, not hers.

Briefly she thought of the life plan she had had. If she were to live, she, too, would live differently. Different college, different major, different friends, even, different future. She had a momentary vision of the campus she had expected to be part of in September. She thought of the college catalog she had memorized, the courses she had signed up for, the campus wardrobe she had begun to plan.

It was not necessary now.

Annabel took the pencil, the envelope, and the paper clips. When they found her body, they would find information. She would make a diary of her death. She would include a letter to Daniel and questions for her father. She would include —

But her body would not be found.

That was the point.

"This is a family matter, Alex," said Emmie. She put her hands on his. He was barely able to keep from jerking his hand away, hers was so cold. It felt like an ice pack. He managed to smile.

"I'm just going in for a second," said Emmie, "to see if there's any news about Annabel or if I can contribute anything. I think they'll just want me to leave. If this is for real, I'm sure they're waiting on the police. So I'll probably be back in a minute and you can drive me home, okay, Alex?"

It was not okay. He had to go in with Emmie.

Alex fidgeted with the keys. Annabel having taken Venice's old Jeep, he and Emmie had taken Venice's new one — a huge, high, loaded Bronco, for bigger and better wilderness driving. Alex was in love with the Bronco. He liked Venice much more for having such excellent taste in vehicles. How easily he'd been sidetracked by the feel of a new car.

Annabel kidnapped . . . I know so much, thought Alex, but I don't know enough. I have to talk to Daniel. His brown Buick is here. I should have cornered him last night but I didn't know how. It threw me, to be with celebrities.

Along with the old Buick, the cars parked around the brick-paved frontage included yet another dark-windowed limousine, a big black van with dark windows, an extremely heavy silver Mercedes, a bright red stunningly gorgeous Porsche.

His eyes fixed on the Mercedes. He knew its owner. He knew every car and every license of that owner.

I left my gun in my own car, he thought. I'm here to kill, and I don't have anything to do it with. I could improvise, I guess. But I'll have only one chance and if I don't pull it off . . .

Emmie reached past his arm resting on the steering wheel and yanked the keys out of the ignition. She didn't meet his eyes but jumped out of the Bronco, throwing a good-bye over her shoulder.

She didn't trust him with the keys? What was she thinking? What did it mean for him?

With fluid grace she ran up the steps and into the Jayquith mansion.

I should get out of here, he thought. I'm in trouble now. Whatever it is I said wrong back during the tennis game, she's thinking of it now.

Emmie had used a sort of credit card to open the gate. The card was clipped beneath the visor. Did he need it to exit or did a movement sensor swing the gate for departure? There was a locking mechanism — Mr. Jayquith had had them closed against his own daughter.

Alex had no keys to start the engine, but the brick drive was downhill. If he put the Bronco in neutral, he could shove from the pavement on the driver's side, leap into the seat as it coasted, and pop-start the engine.

But if he fled, everything ended. He'd never have another chance at his own revenge. Did he want the chance? Did he really and truly intend to follow through on this?

Warm, soft red brick led to safety.

Cold, hard dark marble led to danger.

He was a teenage boy. Danger was infinitely more appealing than safety.

EIGHTEEN

Television crews arrived faster than a summer storm. Gathering at the Jayquith estate, they pressed their faces against the high cast-iron fence and crept under the circling evergreens, hoping to find a way in.

The closed-circuit cameras that recorded movements along the drive reflected faces greedy with excitement. Crowds who habitually gathered at major house fires and bloody car accidents quickly materialized. People who thrived on the trouble and agony of strangers mingled as if at a garden party, hoping something terrible had happened.

A tragedy complete with beauty and romance was revealing itself. They were reveling in it. No stranger at the gate cared about Annabel. They just wanted a big, gory share of the action.

Daniel had spent his life stared at by people lusting to see him cry one more time; people

hoping his mother would have a nervous breakdown in public. People wanted to be sure that
the rich and famous got hurt as deeply as the
poor and anonymous.

Oh, Annabel, thought Daniel. I was pretending you and I could get away from this. We'd
be partners in escape. What has happened to you?
Unless Hollings is a brilliant actor, he's afraid.
His daughter is missing, and he's not in control.
Money to buy the world but not enough money
to know where you are and if you're safe.

Annabel, where are you?

Hollings Jayquith stared at the closed-circuit
TV screen. "Theodora announced it," he said
numbly. "What's the matter with her? A kidnapper buying silence *wants silence*! If this gets
broadcast on television, Annabel is dead."

Annabel dead? Daniel had been haunted by
one death for a decade. Was another to be with
him forever? One laughing girl — dead?

Hollings Jayquith paced. He circled the telephones several times. This was a man accustomed to being in charge the way only dictators
of small countries can be in charge. Dictators of
small countries can order murders, thought Daniel. But do they hurt their own daughters? What
is really going on here?

What if she *was* kidnapped by somebody else?
Daniel asked himself. What if they called The

Camp to speak to me? "Which phone can I use?" he asked Mr. Jayquith. Daniel would like privacy for his phone call, but nothing in this house would be private. He might as well be monitored in person. He dialed The Camp.

Daniel's mother answered in her sweet voice. "Daniel, I don't know where you are. It isn't nice to worry me."

I'm twenty-two, Mother. I've lived away from home since ninth grade. "I'm . . . in Connecticut," he said, postponing the name Jayquith. "Mother, a few hours ago, I got a phone call at The Camp. I have to know if there was a follow-up." He took a deep breath. "Annabel Jayquith has apparently been kidnapped. Somebody telephoned and told me to stay off the networks with our announcement or they'd kill her."

"That black-haired viper who's always in the magazines?" said his mother. "Why would I care if a Jayquith dies?"

"Mother, we're always in the magazines, too."

"We don't have parties in French mansions calculated to snag the world's attention and show off our cleavage. We're living quietly and reasonably at The Camp planning campaigns."

In Daniel's memory, his mother had never been reasonable. He said, "Mother, were there more phone calls?"

"For you?" She was still very sweet. Even calling Annabel a viper she had been sweet.

"Yes, for me." He hung onto his courtesy. Otherwise she would hang up on him.

"No. Nobody has called. What possible connection could you have developed with Annabel Jayquith anyway?"

"We met at the charity ball in the Egyptian Room. I've gotten to know her. Somebody found that out."

"Gotten to know?" said his mother, as if these were disgusting swear words. "You've gotten to know the daughter of your father's murderer? What does *gotten to know* mean?"

He debated how to answer that. He wasn't sure himself what it meant. "Mother, listen to me. I don't want Annabel killed."

In a chilly voice, his mother said, "I didn't want Madison killed, did I?"

His hair prickled.

The lake was silent, cold, and deep. Had Catherine inveigled Annabel off the deep end? Was Annabel's black hair swirling at the bottom of the lake while his mother rocked on the porch and smiled? Was his own mother's voice the whispered tremolo on the phone?

"You need to come home now, Daniel," said his mother.

Whoever had murdered his father had also

half murdered his mother. Taken the goodness and the light out of her, left her bitter and obsessed and easily crumpled. Yes, he needed to go home now. Oh dear God, he thought, what's happening? Please don't let my mother have done anything . . . please let Annabel be all right . . . please, please . . . Formless prayers filled his head. He thought of the pennies he had given Annabel. We shouldn't have wasted our wishes on true love or revenge. We should have wished for long and safe lives.

Daniel set the phone down. "I have to go home," he said.

"And accomplish what?" said Mr. Jayquith.

He couldn't betray his mother to Hollings Jayquith.

Annabel, where are you? Send me a message. I'll catch the thought!

Emmie ran into the room.

Annabel kidnapped. It was impossible. Kidnapping had been a Wythefield in-joke. Whenever a particularly ugly boy appeared at a social event on the campus, somebody was sure to mutter cruelly, "Annabel's kidnapper." Or, if the boy was particularly adorable, "Hey, Annabel. There's a kidnapper for you."

Annabel had been very angry when she left Emmie and Alex in the Jeep. It had not been intelligent of Hollings Jayquith to call Daniel's family pathetic. Mr. Jayquith, when he telephoned Emmie to ask if she'd heard from Annabel, had been hoping the "kidnap" was an extended and stupid joke.

Let it be Daniel and Annabel gone off the deep end with love, Emmie prayed. Because if it's real, I know who has to be involved.

She fought the weakness of tears.

Spread around the vast white living room, like snipers caught in the open, were four furious people. Mr. Jayquith, Mrs. Donavan, Mr. Thiell, and Daniel. No Theodora and no sign of the sudden cousin.

Daniel was wrecked. His shirt was out, his hair sticking up, his face hot and red. His hands were knotted at his sides.

Hollings Jayquith, from his twitching eyes to his pacing feet, was frantic.

"Now, Daniel," Mr. Thiell was saying briskly, like a teacher with a difficult child, "you don't even know Annabel."

There was some truth to that. Those two had skipped getting to know each other. They had gone straight to Love.

"Daniel," said Mr. Thiell, "fond of you as I am, and much as I respect my son's choices in friends, it is impossible to take seriously the ac-

cusations of a boy who plays tennis with the girl
whose father he says killed his. You're the one
with explanations to make! Where have you put
Annabel? What was this call to your mother?
Let's hear from you, Daniel."

"Daniel wouldn't hurt Annabel," said Emmie.

The men were irritated that Emmie would
intrude on their conversation. They glared at
her.

"He loves her. She loves him, I could tell. It
was in their eyes and their walk and the way
they held hands."

Mr. Thiell and Mr. Jayquith rolled their eyes.

"Emmie," said Mr. Thiell, "I'm very fond of
you. We're so proud to have your sister in our
family. But touching as weddings are, there is
no such thing as true love. Certainly not when
the two involved have known each other a matter of minutes. I assume Daniel is using Annabel."

"I am not using her," said Daniel.

No. The girl being used is me, thought Emmie. The answers are sitting in the Jeep. "It's
Alex," she said dully. The lead weight in her
voice stopped them better than clanging cym-
bals. "That's not his real name."

How many years would she weep over this?

She had let onto their grounds and into their homes the very person who had kidnapped her best friend. She had known early on that he was false, and let it go by.

And for what? For a tennis partner.

"His name is Scott Alexander, not Alexander Scott. I read it off his driver's license. He's not anything he says he is."

Face it. She hadn't let Alex pretend to like her, or pretended herself, just to have a tennis partner. She had wanted romance and happy endings. She had wanted to be what Annabel was. Beautiful and surrounded by admirers. She hated herself for wanting these things so much she didn't care if they were trumped up.

Kidnappings were not romantic. They did not have happy endings. Annabel would be killed.

Kidnappers were not kind. They didn't care how much it hurt nor how long it lasted. What pain or personal assault would Annabel endure before her life ended? What terror would her soul and body face before death came like a gift?

My fault, thought Emmie Pearse.

"I thought he wanted my money," said Emmie. When she finished these sentences, she would never want to talk again. She could feel the end of her voice, a few syllables away. "But he didn't even want my money."

Had she really started to love Alex, in so short

a time? She hoped Mr. Jayquith would hurt
Alex, hurt him badly badly badly.

Maybe the pain of this would kill her, too;
they would have a double funeral for her and for
Annabel.

He didn't even want my money, she thought,
let alone me. I was nothing but the door to Annabel. "He's in the Jeep," said Emmie.

Mr. Thiell was out of the room in a heartbeat.
Mr. Thiell's heart was probably the only one
still beating anyway. He flung open the big white
doors and Emmie caught a glimpse of Alex.
Alex, shocked. Alex, slammed back against the
wall by Mr. Thiell's bulk. Alex, trying to shout
her name.

Emmie! out came the word, half-strangled,
half-smothered.

Mr. Thiell kicked the door shut.

The music practice room was entirely empty.
Nor was there a window. That left the basement.

Annabel knew cellars only by repute. She certainly had never had reason to go in one. It
would be filled with spiders and grim, dark, horrible corners and maybe rats or snakes. What's
worse? she said to herself. Rats and snakes and
spiders or getting blown up?

She actually had to think about that one, and
then laughed at herself. Getting blown up is

worse, so go down those stairs and check out the cellar.

There would be no other way out of the cellar, either. She could sit against the doors here in a relatively clean and unfrightening hallway, writing desperately until her lighter died, waiting until she herself died.

She wanted to talk to Daniel about light and dark. About primitive people making the first try at comprehending the world. There was such rhythm to the world. While earth remaineth, said the Bible, seedtime and harvest, cold and heat, summer and winter, day and night, shall not cease.

How comforting. In primitive circumstances you needed to hear that there was a cycle, you would come through on the other side, day would always follow night.

To Daniel she could say, I know why the ancients worshipped the sun. Dark, complete dark, is so terrible. So awe-ful. But there is something even more terrible than dark. Wondering if the people who love you put you in there.

She opened the cellar doors, flashed her lighter quickly enough to see clear steps down to a cement floor, closed the lighter, and went down in the dark. She was just as terrified as she had been the first moment in the dark. Perhaps strange places were always scary, no matter how old you were, no matter how much experience you had.

The cellar was vast. It spread horribly on and on, no doubt beneath the entire stage and auditorium, and perhaps undiscovered building wings as well. It was filled with unknown pieces of large shadowy equipment: Furnaces, she supposed, things to heat with. It was silent as a tomb.

My tomb, she thought.

She came upon a set of steps, wide cement steps going up to a strange flat-lying set of double doors. A bulkhead door, through which to get huge things into the cellar. It was secured by a long steel bar threaded through several large metal hands.

The lighter died.

Annabel clung to the tiny plastic cylinder. She loved the lighter. The lighter had been her only friend and companion. The total dreadful extent of the darkness swirled around her. There was so much more dark down here! It went so far! As if the cellar really extended to the Underground, the Underworld. As if the costumes above her might slide off their hangers, slither down the stairs, and engulf her in their slippery, forgotten personalities.

She wept in the dark. She let go of the worthless lighter and put her hand to her face. Dusty ancient spiderwebs swirled against her skin.

* * *

Theodora arrived amid squealing sirens and screaming tires. She rushed in, distraught but still smashingly effective. Her hair was in place and her earrings were breathtaking. Even Daniel, who noticed jewelry for the first time when he touched Annabel's earrings, was struck by the size and importance of Theodora's trademark.

Theodora was followed by her clone.

Daniel had heard nothing of Jade and was temporarily distracted. Jade was eerily similar to Theodora, but she was less. A watered-down Theodora. Not brass nor bronze. More like a recyclable soda can.

Jade caught Daniel's eye and came over to him. She touched him in the way he most loathed: covetously, as if he were a fine car or sable coat that needed to be stroked before purchase.

Daniel stepped back. He could not suppress a shudder. Jade's eyes turned as blank as a painted mannequin's and she walked out of the room. Theodora hardly noticed. She cried, "My poor Annabel! Hollings, have you heard anything more? She has to be all right! We can't lose her! Who is doing this?"

The phone rang.

Hollings grabbed it, and this time flicked the

controls so that it came over the stereo speaker,
and they could all listen.

But no speech came over the telephone. No
words. Nothing human. Only hot gloating
breathing. A purposeful thrust of breath, like an
alligator in a swamp.

Daniel's hair prickled. A primitive hatred
came right through the phone line.

Mrs. Donavan said, "Very interesting. Everyone wait here a moment please." She left the
room.

Daniel had no interest in waiting. He had been
thrown off by the arrival of Theodora, by the
presence of the creepy little clone, and now he
had to follow up on this Alex thing. Who was
Alex? Who could have hired him? What could
possibly be his purpose in kidnapping Annabel?
Mr. Thiell must be interrogating Alex even
now, perhaps finding out where Annabel was,
and Daniel was standing around listening to
heavy breathers.

He left the room swiftly, Emmie hard on his
heels.

"He's nothing," said Mr. Thiell. But he was
holding a gun on Alex. "I'll dispose of him."

"What are you talking about?" said Emmie.
"You can't dispose of people."

"He was just a gate-crasher," said Mr. Jayquith impatiently. "He wanted your money, Emmie. He has nothing to do with this."

"I have everything to do with this," said Alex evenly, "and so does J Thiell. My brother — "

Mr. Thiell actually lifted the gun, as if he intended to shoot. Daniel's fist smashed down on Mr. Thiell's grip, knocking the gun to the floor. Kill the person who could tell them where Annabel was and why? Daniel felt as if he were wading through a murky rerun of his father's murder; people would keep killing people so that secrets went on being secrets.

"Listen to me, Daniel!" said Alex. "J Thiell killed my brother, Alan Alexander. My brother was a reporter. He was assigned to research Senator Ransom's murder. His paper wanted an in-depth story on the tenth anniversary. He accomplished what nobody else did. He found out the truth. I have my brother's backup disk with his notes. *J Thiell killed your father, Daniel.* J Thiell killed Senator Ransom."

Mr. Thiell merely looked exasperated. His gun lay on the floor. His eyes fastened on it, but he did not attempt to stoop down to get it. He was too slow for that. Two young men would get there first.

"No," said Daniel. "My father was putting together a dossier on Jayquith. He told my mother that."

"On *Theodora* Jayquith, not Hollings," Alex said. "Your father was having Theodora followed because she always went where J Thiell was and she left a much more visible trail than J Thiell. Theodora, the world's top investigative journalist, never investigated her own partner. She never knew it, but all this time, all over the world, the man she loved was evil."

Emmie sucked in her breath. "Partner!" she said. "What was the evil? What was the senator going to expose?"

"J Thiell's cause. The environment. Green space."

Daniel had been thinking of drugs, of money laundering, of arms sales, or nuclear weapons dealing. Those were evil. But — green space?

"He didn't *buy* those factories," explained Alex. "They were his all along. J Thiell hasn't bothered to dispose of toxic waste *ever*. He just stuck it in the ground. The green space stuff, the whole wildlife preserve thing, is nonsense. Just a cover."

Emmie tried to figure out what he was talking about.

"Don't you see? It saved him tons of money to skip disposal costs. And then he took the toxic wastes of anybody who'd pay him enough. All he did was stick it in basements, bury it in meadows. Years and years now. And when people seemed to be gaining on him, he came up with the preserve idea, the high fences, the barbed wire, no humans ever. He even had charity balls to raise money for it." Alex laughed grimly. "For himself, really. Inspecting the records of that so-called charity should be enough to put him in prison."

Daniel turned to stare at J Thiell. The man continued merely to look annoyed. If Alex's accusations meant a thing to him, it didn't show. Daniel could not get interested in green spaces and corrupt charities. "Why would J Thiell take Annabel?" said Daniel.

"Because," said Alex, "if my brother found out about the waste sites, so could other people. If you investigate my brother's murder, the trail leads to your father's murder, Daniel. And don't forget why your father was shot. It was because he was going to expose an entire industry. *What industry?* That's the key. What was Senator Ransom going to say that morning? Whoever killed your father *still* doesn't want his industry investigated."

Daniel studied the gun on the floor. Flat and untouched, it remained menacing. Something like it had ended his father's life. What had J Thiell meant to do with Alex's life?

"Annabel told Emmie and me," said Alex, "that you were going on Theodora's show.

Theodora wouldn't have kept that a secret from
Mr. Thiell! She was thrilled! It was such a coup!
Theodora would even have told him that you
expected to prove who the murderer was."
Wild-eyed, Alex looked briefly at Mr. Thiell and
turned back to Daniel, as if Daniel's opinion,
and only Daniel's, mattered now. "Mr. Thiell
didn't know you had the wrong person in mind,
Daniel. He had no idea you were thinking of
Hollings Jayquith. Of course he thought you
were going to expose *him* . . . Mr. J Thiell!"

"Pathetic," observed Mr. Thiell, looking de-
tached, as if he had never held a gun on Alex,
never thought him a threat.

"I wouldn't put it past Mr. Thiell," said Alex,
"to lay out evidence so that *you'll* be held responsible, Daniel, when Annabel is killed."

"How absurd," said Mr. Thiell. "Why would
Daniel even care if Annabel were taken? How
would a kidnapper ever imagine that Daniel
Ransom could be involved with her?"

"I was at the wedding. At the reception. It
was pretty clear to me how deeply they were
involved." Alex turned back to Daniel. "I think
Mr. Thiell figured that taking Annabel would
stop you from going on the show this week.
And he was right. Meanwhile he'd have her
killed and leave strings of evidence that you did
it. If you murdered the billionaire's beautiful

daughter, you'd lose all credibility. You couldn't convince America that the sky is blue, let alone that you know who murdered your father."

"When Annabel is killed?" repeated Daniel.

"He has to get rid of her to make it work," said Alex matter-of-factly. He had a brother who had been gotten rid of. To him it was simple logic. He said to Mr. Thiell, "I came to kill you. But not with a gun. Guns are too far away. Guns have little pieces of metal to do the work. I want you to admit it. Admit that you murdered my brother. Then I want to beat you to death. With my fists. I want to crush your skull myself."

But the words were tired. The threats of a boy at the end of his rope. A boy too weary to carry them out.

If Alex is right, thought Daniel, Mr. Thiell's money will protect him. We will never reach Mr. Thiell. We won't even be able to get a court order to investigate a single wildlife preserve. Whatever Alex's brother put on his disk, J Thiell will make sure it's not admissable in court. But court is too far away to care about. We have to find Annabel. "Where is she?" he said to Mr. Thiell.

Mr. Thiell shook his head. "Daniel, Daniel. This is a very strung-out young man. Let's not get distracted from the phone calls coming in. We have a kidnapper out there who is clearly going to want a ransom delivered. And only that kidnapper knows where Annabel is."

Who do I believe? thought Daniel. He was unbearably tired. He thought he must look like Alex, who was quivering with emotional exhaustion. Having made the accusation he had so ferociously wanted to make, Alex was no longer ferocious at all.

But Mr. Thiell . . . he still looked ferocious.

Emmie said, "I know where Annabel is."

NINETEEN

The fat woman could not have overheard Jade saying anything, because Jade had not said anything. Just breathed. It had been Mr. Jayquith who talked, who pleaded, who made offers. Jade could hear him in stereo, his shouts coming down the long, bare corridors of stone and through the telephone wire.

But the fat woman was in the Peach Room anyway, fat hands taking the little peach telephone that was Annabel's private line out of Jade's hands. "In your calculations," said Mrs. Donavan to Jade, "you forgot that this is a security conscious house. Every aspect of this house is state-of-the-art. Including telephone security. Did you think you could use Annabel's line to call the main number and we wouldn't know?"

Jade said nothing. What was there to say? It had never crossed her mind that they would re-

alize she was the caller. She had thought herself
vanished and gone once she was out of sight and
down the long halls.

"The numbers came up on the central computer screen. I had only to glance at it to see that
the very phone call terrifying us was being made
from our own building."

She had never had to think more quickly. She
had to redeem this. She had to come out a winner. She could not let Mrs. Donavan, who had
sold her to the O'Keeffes, sell her out again.
Think! thought Jade. Think! You got in the
door, you can't let them kick you out again!
Turn this into something good or lose!

Mrs. Donavan gave her a shove and marched
her back to Theodora and Hollings, who were
hovering over the phone waiting for it to ring
again. It gleamed like scarlet fingernail polish,
full of the conversations it had heard. Theodora
touched her hair as she waited. She was as slick
as the phone itself.

"Excuse me," said Mrs. Donavan woodenly.
"This is your caller." She put Jade in front of
her like an exhibit.

Hollings and Theodora Jayquith straightened
up. How thin they were: that rich kind of thin,
people who had never been inside a kitchen, let
alone rummaged for snack after snack.

"The heavy breathing," said Mrs. Donavan,

"was not a kidnapper. It was Jade using Annabel's line. I suspect previously it was Jade using one of your New York studio lines."

Horrified disbelief invaded Theodora's showy features. "How could you do this, Jade?" she whispered. "It was evil. It was cruel. How could you even think of torturing us like this?"

Jade flung herself forward, hands on hips, eyes wide with rage, trembling. She had wanted to answer that question for so long. She could answer that question for days! "Don't you dare blame anything on me, you hypocrite! How could *you* do this, is the question! You were too busy to bring up your own child. That's your excuse, Theodora. Too busy. You weren't too poor, you weren't too sick, you weren't too abused. You were just too busy. So if you don't like the job the O'Keeffes did, too bad. It was your choice."

Jade had never so totally resembled Theodora. She might be facing three enemies, stronger, bigger, wiser and more experienced, but she was not stopped, she was not even slowed down.

Hollings Jayquith was overcome by Jade's resemblance to Theodora. She could have been the little sister with whom he had fought through childhood over who went first, who got the good swing or the last candy bar. His greatest rival, the one for whom he had built his empire, to show Theodora for once and for all who was first.

In spite of his fear and rage about Annabel, Hollings felt love for this girl who was his niece. And shame.

If he had listened to Annabel, none of this would have happened. But he had been entranced by Jade's uncanny resemblance to Theodora. He had even been entranced by the fakery: the dyed contact lenses, the frosted hair. Theodora had created herself: chosen the blinding earrings, the great flat-brimmed hats, the shotgun laugh. Why should Jade not do the same? Create herself to shock an audience?

"Jade, you may have anything," said Theodora. "Whatever money and home and future you want, it's here. All that matters is Annabel."

Hollings knew immediately the size of his sister's tactical error. All that matters is Annabel? Jade wanted to be what mattered. It was why she had come.

Hatred swept visibly over Jade. "Your dear brother Hollings took Annabel himself, Theodora," said Jade.

"Don't be ridiculous," said Theodora. "Why would he do that?"

"I don't know, but I saw the chauffeur pack her clothes."

"Jade," said Theodora, "this is serious. Don't

lay blame on people who have been loyally employed here for more years than you've been alive. What really happened?"

"How would I know what really happened? You were being a jerk and I took advantage of it."

"Jade!" said Hollings Jayquith. "No more lies. We have to know how deeply you are involved and what it is you're involved in! Who took Annabel? Where is Annabel? What is happening?"

"Either you took her, or she took herself," said Jade.

They went on and on, spitting like cats.

Wasting the only thing they had left: time.

"His wedding gift to Venice," said Emmie. She looked at Mr. Thiell with wrath. "How you must have laughed to yourself at the wedding, Mr. Thiell! There was Daniel Madison Ransom, drinking toasts with you, when you murdered his father. There was my sister, grateful for your splendid generosity, when that gift is going to be where Annabel dies!"

"What are you talking about?" shouted Daniel. He was so tired of half explanations and riddles! *Where is Annabel?*

"My guess is, she's at his next Thiell Wildlife Preserve. There's an abandoned college up in the

mountains. It shut down five years ago and they
were never able to sell the campus. It's remote
and scenic but the roads in are narrow and treach-
erous and nobody would buy it. Venice thought
it was beautiful, the last great space in the mountains. She and Michael went up there to cross-
country ski last winter. When Mr. Thiell asked
Venice what she wanted for a wedding present,
she said she wanted the old college to be made
into a preserve."

"Why would he put Annabel there?" said
Daniel.

"He'll detonate the buildings. That's what he
does. When they're reduced to rubble, he covers
them. Like any other landfill. The college is already fenced in. They'll just beef up the fencing
to keep people out. Not that anybody ever drove
up there anyway."

Detonate the buildings.

Beautiful soft Annabel, blown to smithereens.

Daniel stared at Mr. Thiell, trying to know
what he could believe. Sweet Michael's father
did things like this? Was that possible? But he
had been willing to believe the father of sweet
Annabel did things like this. What was the truth?
How would he ever know?

Mr. Thiell could not resist speaking. Every
American has the right to remain silent, and silence is the most important thing of all. But

silence does not boast; silence does not brag. And even the wisest criminal, like J Thiell, gets tired of silence.

"Actually," said J Thiell, smiling, "it's set on a timer." He looked at his watch. "I believe you're running out of time, Daniel." He chuckled. "Or Annabel is."

It was pointless to hope. The bulkhead doors were certainly, like the doors in the auditorium, chained and padlocked on the outside as well.

But she would try.

Annabel pushed through the hanging webs keeping her spread palms in front of her face. She could handle anything except spiderwebs on her face. She tripped on the steps up and fell painfully. Her cry of pain was swallowed by the basement.

Scrabbling forward, she found the steel bar that kept the bulkhead doors sealed. It was wrapped in wire. The only possible way out — and she would have to peel away the explosive to find out if it opened.

They ran for Emmie's Bronco, Emmie carrying Mr. Thiell's gun and the car keys. All three tried to get in the driver's seat. Emmie didn't argue. She held the upper hand at last. The boys backed off, Alex getting in the back, Daniel in the passenger seat.

Emmie had never actually driven there. But she knew where the turns were. "The question is, can we find Annabel? It was a college, Daniel. There are dorms and classrooms and science labs. An administration building, and a gym . . ."

They would have to push through the crunch of sightseers at the gate. Nose through the crowd hoping people would give way. They would certainly be followed by reporters. Daniel found it unbearable that a parade of cameras and curiosity would snake behind them.

Parked next to the Bronco, waiting in the courtyard, sat J Thiell's men in the big silver Mercedes. As soon as we leave, thought Emmie, Mr. Thiell will come out, climb into the Mercedes, and they'll follow us. If he's the kind of man Alex says he is, the whole trunk of that car is probably filled with weapons. We'll never save Annabel. They'll get there when we do and we'll all sit on the hillside together, and she'll be fireworks in the sky.

Emmie had never driven in her life except carefully and cautiously. It was Venice who drove like a maniac. Venice's Bronco. Her four-wheel drive. The one she planned to take out on the desert and up in the Canadian forests. Emmie had not even driven over; she'd let Alex take the wheel. Her fear of the huge high Bronco had been so great that even when she thought Alex had engineered the kidnapping of her best friend, she wanted him to drive!

When Emmie used to ride horseback with Annabel, they'd ride two abreast. Two horses took up as much room as a Bronco, didn't they? Emmie gunned the engine and the Bronco spurted off the brick drive, right through the deep flower beds and over the lush green grass. Alex was practically thrown out of the backseat and Daniel grabbed both door and dash.

They flew into the forest on the riding trail and the Jayquith mansion disappeared from sight. "This is the way Annabel took when she ran after you!" yelled Emmie. She was gripping the wheel tightly. There was not, after all, quite enough room for the Bronco. Branches scraped and whapped against the windshield. Ditches the horses easily spanned caught the wheels and flung the three occupants into the air. Emmie landed with a jaw-breaking crunch. Twice they had to stop for Alex and Daniel to leap out and tow a fallen branch from the path. They hit a low-hanging branch with such force it took out one headlight and left a spray of red glass on the pristine forest path. The tire marks she left in the soft soil were raw and ugly.

She did not slow down for anything and burst out of the forest on her own road, as Annabel had only that morning, took a left, and headed for the highway. If the silver Mercedes tried to follow them, the low heavy body would get hung up on the first bump and only a tow truck would get it out. And if J Thiell went by normal routes, they were miles ahead of him; he had to go all the way around.

Little twigs of evergreens had caught in cracks of the Bronco. They looked decorated for a camouflage exercise.

Emmie was having fun.

She had loathed Venice for being so daredevil and athletic but it came to Emmie that what she really loathed was that Venice, by virtue of being older, got there first. How many years Emmie had wasted trying to be the opposite of Venice. How many years Venice had had more fun!

Fun . . .

Annabel's being blown up was not fun. Venice and Michael finding out that Michael's father was a murderer was not going to be fun, either.

Venice had meant her wedding vow. For better or for worse. It would get much worse very quickly. But Venice would stay with Michael, and it is easier to face anything when you are a pair. Michael's profile was not worldwide, like Daniel's. It hardly existed. J Thiell never discussed his son, and nobody knew who he was.

Michael will get through it, thought Emmie. Venice will get through it. The question is, will Annabel?

Stars lay in the sky like sequins sewn on velvet. The night sky was a designer dress for a beautiful woman.

A nearly full moon cast a pale, pale light in the dark, dark shadows of the mountains and trees.

Emmie turned sharply to the right and up a very steep hill. A faded college sign had fallen off its post and lay tilted on the grass.

At the top of the hill, the thick evergreens that tightened around the lane burst apart. Below, in a small valley lay the campus. In the moonlight it had charm, quietly awaiting the return of its students. Dorms in which nobody slept on the beds, classrooms in which nobody dreamed, labs in which nobody learned.

The fresh steel of fencing put up around every Thiell Wildlife Preserve glittered out in the grass. Vicious curls of wire had not yet been attached, but lay in packages on the meadow.

The Bronco, however, could not go through. The gate was padlocked.

The boys vaulted out, attacking the gate, shouting Annabel's name.

But the gate was solidly fastened and Annabel did not shout back.

The silver Mercedes crawled up behind them.

The campus lay in silence before them, awaiting its death.

And in which building Annabel lay, nobody knew.

TWENTY

Alex and Daniel were long gone. An eight-foot chain-link fence was nothing. Up and over they went, racing across the bumpy grass, splitting up, Alex heading toward one end of the campus and Daniel toward the other, screaming, "Annabel! Annabel!"

Emmie stayed with the Bronco. Her first thought was that she would drive around the fence to pick them up wherever they came out. But the bumper of the heavy Mercedes pinned her neatly to the fence. The headlights illuminated Emmie briefly and then went out.

She was not, surprisingly, afraid of Mr. Thiell. She did not believe that he would hurt his son's new sister-in-law. But she did not get out of the Bronco, either. She locked the doors as he was getting out of the Mercedes and rolled her window down only an inch.

"Emmie, Emmie," said Mr. Thiell. "A terrible misunderstanding. You must signal your friends to come back. The buildings are wired. Timers are set. Poor Daniel and his confused young companion will be hurt."

The cries of "Annabel! Annabel!" echoed in the dark.

But even if they heard her answer, how could they release her? Buildings about to be blown up are sealed tight. Otherwise some curious ten-year-old boy exploring might be there at the crucial moment.

In his hand Mr. Thiell held a small black object, rather like a television remote control. He was smiling.

It's the detonator, thought Emmie. When Daniel and Alex are close enough to the buildings, he'll touch the right combination. Boom. They're dead. Like a kid's game. Bang. You're dead. But it won't be a game. This man whose specialty is games — whole cities and casinos — he himself does not play games.

"Get out of the Bronco, Emmie," said Mr. Thiell pleasantly. "Or I'll have to touch the controls."

Annabel left the bulkhead door open.
She breathed in huge chunks of air.

Wonderful soft smells of summer filled her.
She could smell honeysuckle and pine. She could
see fireflies.

I'm out.

Fear stayed inside the cellar with the dust and
the plastic explosives. She was standing on real
grass, soft stems brushing wetly on her bare legs.
Compared to the blackness of her imprisonment
the starry night was utterly clear. She gazed upon
the world as if she had been away a thousand
years.

In the end, she had simply hung her whole
weight on the knotted wires until they separated.
There was no current in them and nothing happened. After all that horror and fear, there was
nothing to it. Then she had slid the bar out of
its handle and used her shoulders to press upward
and lift the bulkhead door.

Annabel Annabel Annabel Annabel. The world
reverberated with her name, welcoming her
home.

What time is it? she wondered. Midnight?
Two A.M.? Four A.M.?

Annabel Annabel. Who was calling her? Was
she making it up in the residue of her fear or
were people out there looking?

She had no idea where she could be. Around
her were buildings whose silhouettes in the
moonlight seemed rather formal, as if they

should be gathered about a city square, but beyond them she could see the outlines of the hills.
She could smell the forest.

Headlights penetrated the sky. Far away and
high above, a car had stopped on a hillside. The
headlights went out. Stopping for what reason?
To watch an explosion?

Annabel began to run.

Who? Who? Who?

Who had locked her up? Who was coming to
watch her die?

"Daniel is a very sick boy, Emmie," said Mr.
Thiell to Emmie. She was dwarfed by him and
his two thugs. It terrified her to be standing
among them. But she had no place to go. "He
wanted to take his revenge by killing Hollings
Jayquith's daughter. There's a certain twisted
logic to that. Destroy the person Jayquith loves,
just as Jayquith destroyed the person Daniel
loved. Daniel knows about the wildlife preserves, you see, because he's my son's good
friend. It was really very clever of him to utilize
the buildings."

"Stop it!" hissed Emmie. "You cannot get
away with this! You cannot transfer any blame
to Daniel Ransom! You are responsible for
everything. And if anything happens to Annabel
or Daniel or Alex, I will know."

"Ah, Emmie, you're a young girl whose jealousy of her beautiful older sister is pathetically obvious. Would anyone in authority believe such a sad little case? No. To whom would you carry your little version, Emmie?"

He was right. He would brazen it out. After all — look who would be on his side! Theodora Jayquith herself. Theodora could never allow herself to believe that she had associated all these years with a man willing to murder her beloved Annabel. Willing now also to murder Daniel and Alex. Presidents of countries, CEOs of corporations, Wall Street hotshots — they got away with their crimes; why could J Thiell not get away with his?

"Emmie, Emmie," said Mr. Thiell sadly. "Your poor sister will have to deal with your nervous breakdown when she gets back from her honeymoon. Is that fair to her?"

The high-beam headlights in the Mercedes went back on. Blinded, they swerved to stare. Who could be in the vehicle?

Yellow light like some evil X ray exposed them on the hillside.

"I used your car phone, Mr. Thiell," said Annabel in her high clear voice. "The state police are on their way. Also my father."

Emmie's knees gave way.

Annabel was out. Annabel was safe.

"Give me the detonator, Mr. Thiell," said Alex.

From her new position low in the grass, Emmie saw the two boys appear behind Mr. Thiell's men. Nobody was armed. Nobody had thought it was necessary. They had expected that the boys would get themselves blown up and that would be that. Who needed guns when there were plastic explosives in place?

"You and I, Mr. Thiell," said Alex, "are going in there. I will have the detonator. Once you and I are inside, I'm going to detonate the buildings. Because there's no point in trying to get you through the law. The law will smile on you, the way it always has, because you pay it off, what you don't own already. Nobody knows better than me. My brother Alan — you got away with that. Well, you're not getting away now."

Alex is willing to die, too, in order to get his revenge, thought Emmie. She struggled to her feet and backed away from the group. Annabel was in the Mercedes, Daniel and Alex were facing J Thiell and his two men. The men's eyes were darting, assessing, trying to decide what to do here. Waiting, Emmie thought, for directions from J Thiell.

Or from me, she thought. Because after all, one of them was armed. Emmie Pearse lifted the gun that she had taken from Mr. Thiell back at the country house. "No, Alex," she said. "You won't be a murderer, too. You are a good person. That's the point here. They are the bad guys. We are the good ones."

J Thiell's fingers closed on the small black case in his palm. Emmie would have done the same. Send the buildings up now. Why leave even the slightest chance that Alex would manage to escort him onto the grounds? It wouldn't be a nice way to die.

J Thiell provided them with the greatest fireworks on earth. Black and silent buildings leaped into the sky with color and grandeur and great screaming noise. Metal clashed on metal like a thousand cars crashing.

The explosion ended far more quickly than seemed possible. The night was too dark to see its effect. The stink spread quickly. Baked dust, roasted wood, heated brick.

But no corpses, thought Emmie. The people I care about are alive.

She heard sirens in the distance. Whether or not Annabel had actually reached help on the car phone, help was going to come after the sky lit up like a neutron bomb. Emmie handed the gun to Daniel and ran for the Mercedes. Annabel got out and the two girls embraced. "You're alive!"

whispered Emmie. "Oh, Annabel, I thought maybe — I was so scared for you — it's been awful!"

It had been awful for Annabel. But no longer. She was floating on relief. She would never tell anyone, even Daniel, that she had believed her own father had ordered her death. Of all the secrets of her life, she now had the greatest: She had believed that Hollings Jayquith *was* capable of evil.

Her father was good; he just had bad taste in friends.

Her aunt was good; she had just deceived herself over a man, and what woman hadn't done the same at least once?

Her family loved her. Sidetracked by J Thiell's manipulations and by Jade's arrival. But they loved her.

And Daniel . . . he could love her now . . . he could admit it . . . he could say her last name out loud . . . and stand next to her . . . be joined to her.

Annabel let Emmie spill out emotions. Annabel kept hers.

Up the torturously narrow drive came the first police car, followed by the first rescue truck and the first fire engine.

Daniel put the gun away. He didn't feel like

explaining it to the rescue squads. No sense confusing the issue.

Mr. Thiell and his men retreated to the Mercedes and the four young people stood on the opposite side of the Bronco. None of them was going anywhere, not with those huge vehicles lumbering up that narrow drive.

"There's going to be terrible publicity," said Emmie shakily.

"We've been there," said Daniel. "Publicity is nothing new."

The immensely powerful lights of the rescue vehicles bathed them. Annabel narrowed her eyes to see Daniel. I wonder what my hair looks like, she thought. I don't want a reunion when my hair is disgusting.

She had to laugh. Her laugh caught Daniel and he laughed with her, and ran toward her and caught her in his arms. He kissed her in the dark and they tasted the dust of the explosion. They kissed it away.

"What's new," said Annabel, "is proof. J Thiell is going to jail." She traced Daniel's sturdy profile with her fingers.

"He'll be out in ten minutes with bail," protested Alex. "If the local police even book him. They'll probably book *us*."

"No," said Daniel Madison Ransom. "I'm going to use my name. It's a name that gets done what needs to be done. It's time I stopped pretending I'm not there. It's time I leaned into my name. Shout it out loud. Give interviews. Say my piece. Daniel Madison Ransom *is* somebody. Not just somebody's son.''

TWENTY-ONE

The centerpiece was a sandcastle seven feet high. Slender towers and window slits trembled above moats and courtyards.

Daniel was mesmerized by it. "What's it made of?" he said to Annabel, who didn't know. "I think it's Styrofoam," Daniel said. "The florists designed it like architecture and sprayed sand on it. It is fabulous, Annabel! We're keeping it!" He grinned at her.

"Our first home?" teased Annabel.

Daniel didn't risk answering that one. "Let's dance," he said.

"There's also food. As I recall, you like food even better than dancing."

"Dance me over to the food," said Daniel.

Her dress was pale and frosty, like lemon sorbet. Her wonderful hair was loose and sweetly scented. He turned his cheek against it, savoring the silkiness.

The night of the kidnapping — actually, the morning after; it was way past dawn before they got back to Annabel's country place — Annabel's first priority had been washing her hair. She insisted that nothing more, absolutely not one thing more, could take place until she had showered and washed and dried her hair.

Daniel had loved that.

No confrontations without beauty.

He and Mr. Jayquith did not become buddies while waiting for Annabel to get her hair squeaky clean. It was all they could do to stand in the same room. When Annabel came into the vast white living room where the men waited, her hair black as starry nights, they both walked toward her.

She could hug only one of them first.

She hugged Daniel.

It kept a smile on his face all through the week that followed. Not an easy week. Alex had been right. Mr. Thiell did have presence; every sentence he uttered carried the weight of experience and money and power. All the local police said was, You rich New Yorkers should stop boozing so much at your weddings. Celebrating by blowing up buildings is going too far.

But Daniel's attorneys had arrived. Mr. Jayquith's attorneys arrived. Theodora was told. Duplicates of Alex's brother's disks were booted up on the computers in Mr. Jayquith's office. It was now a matter of time. Justice would follow as it had followed other powerful men, from presidents to Thiells.

How peaceful, after the years in which the death of his father ruled his entire life, to have it solved.

I'm sorry, Dad, thought Daniel, remembering the living father who had tossed him baseballs and taken him skiing. I need to bury it. I need to live. I can't follow in your footsteps, Dad. They're yours. I'm going another way. Please be proud of me.

The party tonight had been Annabel's decision. She said no matter what had gone wrong, they were going on, and they were going on with glad hearts. Both families, she said firmly, were going to get out there in the public eye and rejoice that they were alive and had each other.

Theodora, who had wanted to go into seclusion, was there. Reeling from the shock of J Thiell's ugly life, she still toughed it out.

Jade, who in Daniel's opinion should be shipped in an airless box back to Ohio, was there.

His mother, whose vengeful center had evaporated, leaving her wispy and confused, was there.

Emmie was there, and Scott Alexander,

whom they still called Alex, was there.

No party with those guests could be a success. But it was. Annabel was a demanding hostess. Be cheerful! she ordered. Laugh! Dance! Enjoy!

Over at the food, Daniel found himself next to Mr. Jayquith again. They gave each other the tight smiles of former enemies who had been told by the United Nations (Annabel) to be nice.

"But what about Tommy?" asked Emmie. "He's the one I don't understand at all."

Mr. Jayquith was still shocked over his chauffeur. "J Thiell recommended him," he said, trying to shrug. "Years ago. Tommy was in the front seat listening in on half my telephone discussions! He knew about my buyout difficulties, my merger headaches, my stock option nightmares. I never thought about his presence. He was so much furniture. All along he was selling information to J Thiell."

"But I always thought Tommy liked Annabel and me," said Emmie.

"Tommy claims he didn't know what was planned for Annabel. He insists that he was told she was going to be locked up for a few days until things cooled off. I'd like to believe him, but I don't."

How much would any of them believe other people's stories now? How much could any of them trust or relax in the future?

"What happens to Jade?" Annabel said quietly to her aunt.

Jade was dancing with one of the television people in Theodora's train of admirers. She was not wearing a dress of Annabel's. Theodora had taken her to a shop whose one-of-a-kinds were legend. Jade did not look like a legend. She looked like the daughter-of-a-legend.

Theodora remained expressionless, which was unlike her. For television she had learned large, camera-ready expressions. "Jade needs a wider horizon. I think the United States is too confining for her. There's a delightful program for students on an ocean liner: classes on board ship while sailing to ports from Portugal to Hong Kong. Jade will be gone ten months, seeing the world. When she comes back, we'll see what kind of woman she is. I want to believe that the temptations of money overcame her. I want to believe she is a decent person."

We want to believe everyone we know is a decent person, thought Annabel. But it wasn't money that overcame Jade. Aunt Theodora is still deceiving herself. Hate motivated Jade, and the hate is still there, waiting like revolution, to come out from under the dictatorship.

Annabel was relieved that Jade would vanish for ten months, but she wondered if that was wise. Jade would know that she was literally

being shipped off. Just as Jade, dancing across
the room, knew that the Jayquiths were talking
without her, a group the excluded her . . . that
always would.

Daniel turned Annabel's cheek to face him.
Annabel forgot her sudden cousin.

Emmie had eyes only for Alex, who was talking to Mr. Jayquith. Alex had used Emmie
and still she adored him. Alex's list of things to
do and people to meet began and ended with
avenging his brother's death. He had come to
the party only to discuss the next stage in pros-
ecuting J Thiell.

Emmie had so completely lost her heart in so
short a time. Losing your heart turned out to be
terrifying. You could lose it, as Theodora
Jayquith had, to a friend who brutalized your
own family.

Say good-bye, thought Emmie. Don't show
emotion. Don't even have emotion. Just check
Alex off as experience.

Emmie had talked to Venice by phone. Not
only would Venice weather this, she would
flourish in the face of this adversity. This was
thunder and lightning, sleeping out in the storm,
laughing in the face of nature. Venice and Michael were going to be all right.

Halfway through the evening, Alex thanked

her for her assistance in a difficult time. He appreciated Emmie's understanding, he said, and he hoped she didn't hold it against him.

"I do, actually," said Emmie. "I think there were more direct and less hurtful ways to do what you were trying to do."

Alex did not know what to say to that. "Take care of yourself," he said finally. He waved good-bye, although they were only a foot apart.

"You, too," she said quietly. Alex left the room and her life, while Emmie forced her heart to shrug. If I'm going to take care of myself, she thought, I'd better do a decent job at it.

She crossed the room and tapped Gavin on the shoulder.

"Hey, Emmie," he said, glad to see her. Genuinely glad. Maybe they've always been glad to see me, she thought, and I never bothered to look. "Hey, Gavin. Let's dance."

"Or talk?" offered Gavin plaintively. "Dancing wears me out."

"You're everybody's dance partner at these things," she said, surprised.

"I know. That's why they invite me. I'm a good sport. But I'd rather talk any day. Tell me about your college plans. Engineering, isn't it?"

He had remembered. That surprised her. Well, maybe there were more surprises in store for her. Nice surprises.

* * *

Daniel's hand lay on Annabel's waist, as it had in the Egyptian Room, warm and heavy and sure of itself. Annabel took his big hand between her smaller ones, making an envelope of her fingers.

We hardly know each other, she thought. And my heart and mind are convinced that he is not only decent, but absolutely wonderful . . . and meant for me.

If I had another penny, I would make another wish.

That the next promise will be no secret. It will be in front of our friends. A vow to love and to cherish forever and ever.

You have only just become acquainted with the Jayquiths, Daniel Madison Ransom. So let me tell you something about us.

We get what we want.

About the Author

Caroline B. Cooney lives in a small seacoast village in Connecticut, with three children and two pianos. She writes every day on a word processor and then goes for a long walk down the beach to figure out what she's going to write the following day. She's written about forty-five books for young people, including *Flight #116 is Down*, *The Party's Over*, *Saturday Night*, *Last Dance*, *Summer Nights*, and *The Cheerleader*.

Ms. Cooney also plays the piano for the school music programs, enjoys doing embroidery, and reads a mystery novel a night.